A Loving, Faithful Animal

Josephine Rowe

 Catapult · New York

Copyright © 2016 by Josephine Rowe

First published in Australia in 2016 by University of Queensland Press
All rights reserved

First published in the U.S. by Catapult (catapult.co) in 2017

ISBN: 978-1-936787-57-9

Catapult titles are distributed to the trade by
Publishers Group West
Phone: 866-400-5351

Library of Congress Control Number: 2016952069

Printed in the United States of America

9 8 7 6 5 4 3 2 1

For N.

Here's the house with childhood
whittled down to a single red tripwire.
Don't worry. Just call it horizon
& you'll never reach it.
Here's today. Jump.

—Ocean Vuong

A Loving, Faithful Animal

I

A Loving, Faithful Animal

THAT WAS THE SUMMER A SPERM WHALE DRIFTED SICK INTO the bay, washed up dead at Mount Martha, and there were many terrible jokes about fertility. It was the summer that all the best cartoons went off the air, swapped for Gulf War broadcasts in infrared snippets, and your mother started saying things like *I used to be pretty, you know? Christ, I used to be brave.* But you thought brave was not crying when the neighbor girl dug her sharp red fingernails into your arm, until the skin broke and bled, and she cried out herself in disgust. You were still dumb enough to think that was winning.

It was around the same time that your uncle Tetch started turning up in the garage. You pulled up the roller door on the morning of New Year's Eve to get your bike, and there he was, standing barefoot next to the oil stain that your father's car had left behind. Everything in the garage had been made very neat, so it looked like the sort of garage they'd show in a hardware catalog.

Careful, you warned Tetch. There's redbacks galore in here.

I know, he said, and held up one of his shoes to show the mess of spider on the sole.

Just here for my bike.

Tetch went over to the wall and wheeled it out.

I fixed the bell, he said, and he rang the bell to prove it.

There was something a bit wrong with Uncle Tetch, this was the general opinion. But there was something a bit wrong with everyone: your sister, Lani, couldn't keep her legs together, and you had this knot in your chest that nothing could untie. People assured you that it was only growing pains, that it would loosen soon enough, but it just got tighter and tighter. And then there was Belle, poor pup. What happened to Belle wasn't fair.

When your father left—the first week of December, freckles resurfacing across cheeks, the stink of insect repellent suffocating the kitchen—Aunt Stell sent a card that said *It Is Better to Have Loved and Lost Than to Live with a Psycho Forever.* Your mother liked it so much she put it up on top of the fridge, and it stayed there all through Christmas, the smallest of her small revenges, roosting amidst the cards with snow and camels and reindeer.

The card is still up there, standing lonely and a bit proud after the frantic de-Christmasing of the house. You and your sister have spent the morning winding tinsel and fairy lights around your fists, scraping fake snow off the windows, with Lani asking, Why. The fuck. Do we always have to do this?

Mum doesn't even look at her. Because you know why, she says. Because it's bad luck to leave them up. Ru isn't complaining, are you, Ru? (You aren't.)

Lani lets the paint scraper fall to her side. Ha, she says. *Luck.* And Ru's not complaining, because she's got nothing better to do. Shouldn't a kid her age have hobbies?

It sounds parroted, the way she says it, has obviously come from someone higher up. Grandma Mim maybe. You have hobbies. They just aren't for show.

Ru has a vivid interior world, don't you, love? Mum quoting your art teacher, wholesale.

Your sister shakes her head and goes back to attacking the canned frost.

Keep pushing me, girl. See just how far it gets you. Ru, honey, can you give me a hand with these Santas?

I don't know why we even bothered, Lani says, only for you to hear, as you climb down from a chair to take charge of the ornaments.

She's right—aside from the bike, Christmas Day was the same tired cracker jokes and picking at a cold Safeway chook while the TV murmured to itself disconsolately in the living room. Lengths of red and gold tinsel wound around the antenna only made things worse.

But you keep your mouth shut. Let them scrap it out. Let them go at each other like cats, if that's what they want. As soon as you finish tucking the old mercury-glass Father Christmases into their crumbling Styrofoam coffins, the day will be your own.

Now Uncle Tetch stands in the garage and watches you push the bike over the blond stubble of summer lawn. It's obvious he's never cared much for the name Tetch, though he never whinges about it. You try to remember to call him Les, but it isn't easy.

Okay, your mother said once. So Tetch doesn't have your father's brains. But he doesn't have his meanness either.

He's a little younger than your father, and he only has eight fingers—he got rid of both the index ones so he wouldn't have to go to Vietnam. *Can't pull a trigger without a trigger finger.* Most people think that the finger thing must mean he's a coward, but your mother said she didn't know what kind of coward would whip his own fingers off with a band saw or what have you. But his birthday hadn't even come up in the ballot, so who knows what he was thinking.

He's harmless, though. Wouldn't kill a thing but to put it out of its misery, the way he'd done with a fox once, a little one crazy with mange. These days he probably just wants to be useful, hovering around the garage, repairing bicycle bells and such. You didn't ask him for anything at Christmas, but he'd sprung for a secondhand Malvern Star, licked with a fresh coat of bottle green, no childish junk cluttering the spokes. It is the best nonliving thing you've ever owned, and you guide it one-handed, resting your palm between its handlebar horns as though it were a loving, faithful animal, as Dad would say of Belle. Still too sick-making to think of the shreds of fur scattered through the backyard, right down to the fence line, the way you might see from a mauled rabbit or a possum, but never a dog. That was the last family activity, the four of you searching through the grass like an awful treasure hunt. It was Dad who found the ear, all on its own beneath the magnolia. The silky fur so perfect you almost wanted to speak into it, as if she might be able to hear how badly she was missed. Dad picked the ear up, very gentle. He held it in his palm and looked down at it, and you saw his shoulders shake, which was something his shoulders had never done. Then he turned around quick and stalked back to the house. He'd found Belle under the Pyalong Bridge when she was only tiny.

Maybe a fox got her. So said Karlee Howard, of the sharp red fingernails.

Nup, she would've walloped a fox.

You know what it was. Sure you've seen it, crouched black amidst the sea of high yellow grass, keeping its belly to the earth. It slips easily from the rifle sights of farmers, of roo-shooting boys. Is only ever caught in the outer millimeters of grainy film—a lanky shadow and a flick of tail. Scientists and game hunters have come in pursuit of it, set up with tents and traps. The creature is too crafty, outsmarting their snares, walking so lightly it seldom leaves prints. The researchers carry back nothing but samples of grass and hair, tissue from the torn bellies of savaged pets. *Evidence inconclusive.*

Panther is what the locals call it.

You know that it is not your father's panther, the one that came during the war, packed up in a crate from Sumatra after its mother had been shot out of fear or fun. A panther lives twenty years if it's lucky, and that Sumatran cub was not lucky—obviously—getting itself orphaned and then caught, smuggled back to Australia and a lonely life of mascotting at the Puckapunyal barracks. It must've got weak, got bored there on the base, caged up. Wondered where its own kind were, when they were going to come for it. It must've been afraid of the night criers, strange shrieking birds and booming owls, the roaring of bull koalas, languages it didn't understand. Meanwhile, its silhouette was stenciled onto everything that didn't move, and some things that did: your father's arm, for instance. When you were little, the tattoo panther was sleek and wonderful, clawing its way up his bicep. Dad could make it writhe, make it roar. But as the war grew further and further away, the ink faded, softening and spreading at the edges, so that the cat was bigger than it had been but less ferocious, the muscles that moved beneath it growing tired and ropy.

What happened to him?

Our mascot? Got too big, love. Friendly and dopey as a Labrador, but he had to go. Sent to live in a zoo up north.

As for whatever got Belle—that other something, sneaking into backyards for a taste of cat or chicken, fed up with marsupials and disease-ridden wild rabbits—Mum said she'd have it for a throw rug before she let it have her angoras. She protected the rabbits from meeting the same grisly end as Belle, hauling the hutch up to where she could keep an eye on it at all times. Sometimes patrolling the fence at the back of the property of an evening, beyond which all was paddocks and dense banks of blackberries and whatever they might shelter.

Your bike muscles aren't up to much yet, so you stand for the dusty rises in the road and march on the pedals, the sun slung across your bare shoulders, as warm as Reef oil. And although your lungs are on fire and the corners of your eyes are filling with grit, that tight place in your chest is cracking open, the bright afternoon spilling in. The new year will be better. It will be. It will. There's a song on a tape someone made for your sister, and it's playing over and over behind your eyes. Even when it gets so steep that you have to jump off and push, the song is still there—about a wide-open road and how you can go anyplace you want to.

The road levels out where the new estate is going up. It's good, some days, to walk around there, to climb onto the skeletons of roofs or to wander around all those rooms where nothing has happened yet. The Howards are building up there, a bigger place. A poolroom and two bathrooms and bedrooms forever. That's where Karlee tested your nerve.

She's off-limits now. Mum had spotted the little sequence of scabby crescent moons near the inside of your elbow, as though a strange creature with strange teeth had bit there.

Who did that to you? she demanded. Why on earth did you let her? Disfigure you like that.

You hadn't cried out or anything, had stood perfectly still in the room that Karlee said would soon be her bedroom. Felt her breath puff on your cheek as she watched your face for a hint of flinch. Nothing. She dug harder and then too far. It *had* felt like winning, watching her jerk her arm back and scrape under her fingernails. But then she said, Now try me, holding her arm out, and you quit. You had nerve, but only one kind of nerve.

You push on farther, past the ruined hayshed where Matthew Collins got his fingers into Renee Tillman and where the old dredge and dragline is crumbling into the ground like a dead mastodon. On to where the bitumen turns to gravel, shifting loose under the tires, and then the gravel gives way to corrugated dirt, juddering your teeth. Then there's only the three long strips of road, paddock, sky, waving like a tricolor flag, and it's as though no time passes, like sleeping without dreams or dreaming awake, until the road runs out in crooked star pickets and snarls of wire. You heave the bike over and push it through the thirsty grass to a huddle of cypress rising out of the grasshoppers and dust, a quiet green island. Cicada husks cling to the cypress bark, and you try not to crush them, propping the bike against a trunk and crouching down among the needles, untucking a leather pouch from the waistband of your shorts. When your father left, he forgot to take his cigarette things— papers and filters and matches, tobacco that smells sweet like port wine. You got to them before your mother did, before Lani, because you know this much: cigarettes are a kind of power. A kind of toxic magic that can be both the spark of an argument and the end of one. They are more important than milk, than bread, than uniforms or tuition fees. You learned these things early, going to school each morning in clothes that were almost right, clothes that were clean at least, the right colors. But the missing school emblem was a marker in itself: *poor*. Nothing you could do about that except to get mean or stay quiet. Lani had already taken the first option.

You know how much tobacco to pinch from the packet, have watched Dad rolling them up at the kitchen table, somewhere else in his mind. Somewhere far away from Sunday morning, far away from instant coffee and toast crusts. Fat cigarette times and thin cigarette times—three days from pension day, Dad rolled them as skinny as twigs. These might as well be fat cigarette times, you reckon, the tobacco already cut as it is with dried curls of orange peel to give it back some life. You roll one thick as a pencil and lick the gummed edge to seal it. A bit lumpy. Not perfect, but it will do.

From the dark, secret shade of the pines you'll see someone coming long before they see you. Unless that someone gets down on their stomach and slithers through the grass, which they just might. But it's snake season, and that would be, in

Dad's words, about as clever as a box of hammers. Right before he left, he'd promised a trip to the ocean to see the whale, before they figured out how to get rid of it. Neither you nor Lani had ever been close to one, living or dead. Living would be better, but the dead one would do for the meantime. There it was on the news, this wonderful thing the sea had coughed up. They were deciding whether to blow it up, or bury it, or tow it back out through the heads. There was still time. Tomorrow or the next day, Dad said. We'll go. But then came the trouble with Belle, and the morning after that, the car was gone, along with his duffel bag—a sure sign that this stint was going to be another long one—and from the couch you watched as they tied orange ropes around the whale, using cranes to nudge it back toward the water.

The cigarettes are your own revenge, or maybe they are something else: a come-here-you, like a fox whistle. Something that will call your father back in spite of himself. Touch the lit match to the paper, draw deep, don't cough. Don't cough. And he'll come striding up the yellow hill to slap your face. That would be the least worst thing. And still, it doesn't happen.

What have you been given to miss? More than you'll likely remember. More than the smell of pine resin and diesel. More than tooled-leather gimcracks with your name stamped in, and creatures fashioned from wine corks and Easter-egg foil—projects to keep his hands and mind placid. More than being hoisted up for a better view of the moon rabbit; more than the names for constellations and seven slang words for *horse*. More than *this is how to eat a prickly pear* and *this is how you hypnotize a budgie* and *this is how to stave off thirst*—breaking a button from his shirt and sucking on it like a lozenge. More than knife tricks and old wives' tales and nonsense riddles—*why is a mouse when he spins?* He's never read aloud from any book you can recall, has all his poems and songs and jokes stashed away by heart, to trot out whenever the occasion might call for one.

Your father. His head is a ghost trap. It's all he can do to open his mouth without letting them all howl out. Even so, you can still see them, sliding around the dark behind his eyes like a Balinese puppet show. At night he'll let his guard down. Too bad for everyone. Now he's out there somewhere. Wasting his New Year's Eve in a shabby, forgetful room that has bedsheets for curtains, a mattress soaked in other men's fevers. You've seen those rooms. How is that better than being at home? Those sad, seedy places that Mum has dragged him out of before, you and Lani waiting in the car. Bored brainless in the backseat, sucking barley sugar, reading stolen doctors'-waiting-room magazines— "20 Ways I Beat the Change!!"—not understanding how she always hunted him down eventually. Not understanding why she hunted him down at all. Weeks of nothing; then the phone would ring one morning with a tip-off and she'd be thrown into action. Saying, Forget about school, I need you both today. Needed for what, exactly, neither of you could say—to hold on to a fistful of change for the parking meter, keeping watch for the inspector? She'd do her lipstick in the rearview mirror and fluff up her hair—*Okay, girls, cross your fingers*—before clipping up the stairs of a mean-looking building.

Silly bitch, Lani would say after Mum had been swallowed up by the rooming house. It's so embarrassing; he's just going to belt her around again.

Watching your mother in those moments, with her clotted mascara and worn-down heels, it was impossible to imagine her ever being young, impossible to imagine swimming trophies and a modeling portfolio with Vivien's. Most of the proof of that life was elsewhere—pawned or held ransom *up north*, which meant *the house I grew up in*, which meant *grandparents*. These people who were only feathery handwriting on birthday and Christmas cards, padded envelopes containing presents of glittery stationery and books you'd read years ago. The word *Merewether* crouched in the return address like a dangerous spider. *That Merewether mansion*, Dad called it—though it wasn't, Mum insisted, really wasn't a mansion—that's where everything was.

All she had to show now were an arctic fox coat and a photograph of her in the driver's seat of the famous green Corvette a few years before she sold it to pay off a loan. The Corvette is gleaming, cicada-colored, its cream panels like wings and the soft top folded down. You're there, a slight swell under her orange caftan, baby Lani sitting up in her lap like a doll. In the photograph, you cannot tell what is coming. And neither can she. She is laughing behind her Audrey Hepburn sunglasses, oblivious to the time when she will use them to hide bruises and nights without sleep.

This is Exhibit A in the Museum of Possible Futures, the life that might have rolled out smooth as a bolt of satin if she had just swung her slender legs up into that beautiful car and driven as fast as she could in the opposite direction, leaving the man with the camera far behind. Your father, he could keep the photograph.

But she did not drive away. Instead she sold the car and spent every night of her life trying to lead your father out of the jungle, out of the mud, away from the cracks of invisible rifles, strange lights through the trees.

When Lani was five or six, old enough to understand what the shouting meant when you did not, she would climb into your cot to curl around you like a shell—*Big C little c*—and tell you it would be over soon. She'd hum whatever songs she could think of—advertising jingles, songs she'd learned in school—to drown out the shattering of plates, the thud that might be your mother's head hitting the wall. Then it was you climbing into your sister's bed, welcome for a year or two. Top to tail, sardines on toast, till she got tougher and her comforting was something you had to trade for, something to buy with money or favors, her share of the dishes. Then there was nothing you had that she wanted (*I don't even read those stupid vampire books anymore, dumb-arse*), and she said she was tired of waking up with your fricken' feet in her fricken' face. Eventually you became too old for that kind of comfort anyway and, at twelve, too proud. That's how it went.

There is a picture you have in your mind, though you're not certain how it got there. Another photograph from the green Corvette years, maybe, but this one is in black and white: a semicircle of scraggly men standing around a large pit. Looking at the photograph, you cannot see the men's faces. Only their backs, their arms loose around each other's shoulders. You cannot see what is in the pit. But somehow you know what is in there and wish you did not. In the foreground, a pair of rifles are crossed, jabbed barrel down into the dirt, making an X. One of these rifles is your father's. This is all you know about the war, this and the panther and your mother's face.

•

After three fat cigarettes, your brain feels padded with smoke, the afternoon humming with a loud, high-pitched heat. You scuff the fallen pine needles into little heaps with the heel of your shoe. Sometimes there are things left up here—beer bottles, bones, burned pieces of hose, once a pair of grubby cotton knickers tangled in a checkered blanket—so you know it isn't only yours, this place. But today there are just the shells from the cicadas, who have six weeks to fly around, make noise, and have sex before they die—a rotten deal after spending seven years underground, doing nothing.

Mum has a collection of them lined up along the kitchen windowsill, which Lani thinks is creepy as hell. Aunt Stell agrees, says she can't stand to look at them, marching along with their slit-open backs. They make her feel itchy. But Mum thinks they're lucky. For her, the entire world is split into lucky and unlucky, you and your sister included. Lani's birthday is the fourth (unlucky), and yours is the twenty-first (lucky). It's a certain amount of responsibility, this luckiness, looking after it as though it might wear away or stretch thin with your growing.

There are more cicada husks up in the higher branches, an easy climb even with the headful of smoke. Seven is a good number. They don't give up their hold of the tree bark without a fight, and some of them lose a leg or two. But their remaining hook-feet catch in your T-shirt's soft cotton, and they cling there as if they know and trust you anyway.

Riding in the bent green arms of the pine, you want to find a way to keep it all, to press it flat like a gum blossom between the pages of a heavy book, the paddocks and huge sky with the final hours of December dissolving into it. When you close your eyes, it's there for a moment, perfect, but then the edges go fuzzy and it drifts away. After a while it all hurts to look at, too glaring and too empty, and no way to stop the afternoon from running out.

You light another smoke and let the match burn down to make a midget charcoal pencil. Inside of the matchbook for a canvas.

In art class you draw habitats. Not landscapes; habitats. Places that are waiting. Places people or animals might eventually wander into if you can make them seem inviting enough.

Very elegant, those trees, those hills, says Miss Dawes. But don't you think it would all look nicer with some sheep or something?

They'll come later, you tell her. Something, but not sheep. Sheep always look like parasites from far away.

Parasites?

Yeah, like ticks. Or fleecy lice.

I've never noticed that. But you're allowed to use the whole page, you know? There's stacks of paper back there, you don't have to crush it all into a corner.

Okay, you tell her, though you like to keep things small enough to scribble out, small enough to take back, if you need.

She leans in close to study the fine cross-hatching on a copse of ghost gums, whorls of night air like the feathery dark hair at her nape, pasted down now with sweat. What do you know about yourself in these moments? Breathing her smell of forest, of cool earth, her hands stained from slapping out hunks of damp clay on a stone slab. Meant for coil pots, the clay. But the boys will roll theirs out into stumpy cocks, slimy from the work of their sweaty palms, to chase girls around the room. Barely older than Lani, Miss Dawes, but she never yells. Just wonders aloud how come the anatomy is so well observed. Makes the blood roar up to their idiot faces.

How about horses? she whispers conspiratorially. Galloping her hand across your page. Like you're a child.

Maybe horses, you say, looking at her hand. Eventually.

A vivid interior world, she writes. But maybe she writes that for everyone she doesn't understand.

You rip the last match across the striker strip, turn it back on the matchbook, and let the flame eat the sketch. Nothing ever turns out looking true.

A hot wind shakes your tree, the last northerly of the year. It came from inland, from the desert, and it will keep blowing on down the Hume Highway, on into Melbourne, collecting firework smoke and radio countdowns and half-cooked resolutions on its way to the ocean, emptying it all out over the Bass Strait. Everything feels like the last, the very last, as though it's the end of the century and not just the end of the year. The end of the world. That's why everything alive down there in the grass is singing its insect heart out.

Then there's dust rising from over near the road, visible before the motorbike engine is heard, thin and waspish above the silvery cricket whir. The bike rips along the channel of chewed-down grass that runs alongside the fence. William Somebody. Healy, the mechanic's son. His bike isn't made for the country, and the girl hugging his back isn't dressed for riding. She's wearing his helmet, but her arms and legs are bare, and the dress she has on is made of something wet-looking and slinky, a spangled black that's scrunched up high on her thighs.

It's easy to tell, even this far away, that it's Lani. The dress isn't her dress, she must've borrowed it, and with the cherry-red helmet she looks like a doll that's had its head swapped with an action figure's. Inside there, it will smell like sweat and unwashed hair, cigarette breath and cheap aftershave.

If she turns her bobblehead toward the pines, she'll see your bike leaning helpless against the foot of the tree. She'll know you're up there, *Sneaky little shit.* She won't be able to climb up and whack you, not in those shoes. But she can be as mean as cat spit, has a sixth sense for knowing what will hurt most. Looking down at your bike, the sleek almost-newness of it, you wonder how fast could you ride. Not fast enough. Nothing to do but hold your breath, scratchy pine bark biting into your skin while you wait for your sister to see or not see.

There is so much you could tell on her. Before Christmas, she came and cut an L-shaped slit into the flyscreen of your bedroom window so she could sneak in and out at night. *Mum won't check your room, fuckface.* And there are the pills she sneaks from Dad, the ones that are meant to keep him calm, which she sells to people at parties for two dollars a pop. And now this.

You tell, she's said, I'll tell.

Tell what?

You know, she answers, bluffing—what could she know?—but it's better safe than sorry.

Lani and the boy pass right by, like a dream made of petrol fumes and churned-up grass.

You're not the only one in the world. You say it in your mind, and then you say it again right out loud because she won't be able to hear: You're not the only one in the world. But your sister sails out to where the night is reaching its pink claws into the sky, and you know that soon enough she's going to leave this place without you.

After the sound of the engine dies away, you climb down, putting a hand on your bike as though to reassure it. A couple of the cicadas have been crushed, and you brush away what's left of them. Flakes of translucent carapace, still-clinging legs. Sorry sorry sorry, though they wouldn't have felt a thing, wherever their new bright bodies are. And five's okay. Five's still lucky. They hang on the front of your T-shirt like ornaments, riding along that way as you coast home through the last of the light.

Years from now, you will try to explain it. Lying on your back in someone's bed, attempting to shape it with your hands so that they might be able to see you better. How sometimes—in these liminal hours, in the near dark that falls between dog and wolf—you could see past your father's shoulders. Past the crossed rifles and the men who stood in miserable exhaustion around the edge of the pit. You could see right into the silver and the light that moment was made of, to bodies piled on bodies. Limbs in the bulldozed dirt showing like the pale roots of monstrous trees.

You will throw shadows on the bedroom wall, reaching up toward the high pressed-tin ceiling, trying to make yourself understood. And when it's obvious that this will not be possible, that you do not have the words or even the shapes of the words, you will let your hands fall back to the mattress. Birds shot from the sky. You will allow them to be held.

I don't, you will say, want to talk about it anymore. Because you still will not know how. How in such moments you could see past your father's shoulders yet could not see his face.

When you pull up the roller door, Tetch is for once not standing there offering to fix anything. The house is dark and airless, no sound but the refrigerator and the fish tank filter murmuring to each other in their secret electrical language. The sifting of posters as they shed from the walls, from their sweating adhesive. At the table you carefully detach your cicada passengers, raiding Lani's nail polish to give them glossy coats of armor, shellacking them in gold, pale pink, electric blue before lining them up along the kitchen windowsill with the others so that Mum can be surprised the next time she does the dishes. Out there in the yard, she's pulling up handfuls of thistles and having words with the rabbits. Giving them a frozen drink bottle wrapped in an old tea towel so the hutch will stay cool. From inside the kitchen you can't hear the exact words she's saying, but you can tell she's using her phone voice, her best voice, the one she uses when she wants people to respect her. People or animals, whoever's listening. The rabbits, who have both been given various names—Raffles, Shuffles, Wombat, Houdini—now spend every night up on the back porch, hidden under a green tarpaulin weighted with paint cans.

Try asking her what it is she talks to them about—how much can a person have to say to a rabbit?—and she'll just make a joke out of it:

I tell them to mind their own peas and kumquats.

Tonight you'll sit and watch the fireworks on TV—silver birches, Catherine wheels, skyrockets lighting up the banks of the Yarra River, and the golden faces of people oohing about it. The distant bubble-wrap pop of explosions that'll make you want to run to the windows and look.

Too far away, Possum, Mum will say. A name she hasn't used since you were little, and you won't be sure whether this means things are worse or better than they seem.

During the crowd shots you'll search the upturned faces for your father, though you know he won't be there, how he hates crowds. Mum will fall asleep in the armchair, her hand around the phone, and hours later Lani will climb in through your window, her red mouth all blurry and her eye makeup gone panda.

Your father's nightmares will be out of the house—finally, finally—but for a few weeks yet the three of you will wake up and wait for them anyway. Drifting around the house like lost ships: *Go to bed. You go to bed. Don't get smart.*

Some nights, in place of proper dreaming, you'll open the curtains and look out across the darkness. Imagine yellow eyes staring back, a dusky shape slinking through the paddocks, along the windbreaks. Snuffling out the scent of your father and following it to wherever he is, straight down the highway, all the way to the city. Padding between the tramlines while everyone else is asleep.

II
The Coastal Years

WELL, I WAS PRETTY. I DID USE TO BE BRAVE. I'M TELLING YOU.
Skinny as a whippet—you could put your hands like this around my
waist—and just that fast. Wipe that look off your face, girl. I'm tell-
ing you. Before I met your father. Before I . . .

Yes, she can hear herself. Whine whine whine. Evelyn wraps
pale ivory tissue around a trio of flock deer, their taupe fuzz wearing away in patches, giving them a look of hereditary mange. If
she can only get the girls to see. See her differently. Just exactly as
she had been—that's hardly demanding a great stretch of the
imagination; there are photographs, after all. Then she might be
able to see herself that way. Step right back up into her old joy, her
old hope, some large, bright room in herself that's been closed off
these past seventeen years. That could be the start. Of something.
But Ru is unconvinced, and of course Lani won't even try.

With the family of deer safely nested in the box, she tapes
shut the lid. The last of it, though Jack's brother came by hours

ago to help waltz the naked Christmas tree out of the house, and the fallen needles threaded themselves into the weave of the stubby carpet, a trail leading from living room to front door. These too will have to be gone by midnight, every last one, or who knows what. Evelyn hefts the candy-striped Christmas box and follows the path of needles out of the house, bumping the screen door open with a fleshy hip.

The heat, the light today. There's something about it. Here she is, stranded, miles inland, but still it calls up the sandstone coast of her youth. The stickiness of that salt air as she walked toward the ocean baths, to the pool cut right into coastal rock. Every summer morning of her teens and into her twenty-first year. Drifting home with seawater drying on her skin, leaving delicate scuffs of salt dust fine as baking soda beneath the fine blond hair on her arms.

But then maybe it isn't the heat, isn't the light; maybe it has more to do with Jack being gone, maybe for good this time. And this is how she knows, somewhere deep down, that it's for good. His absence whipping the years out from underneath her, like that party trick with the tablecloth, the dishes clattering back not quite as they had been, and she'll have to go back to trying to be whoever she was before the table was set. Whoever she was before he scooped her up out of the ocean baths that last time. Told her, This is it, Kiddo, today's the day, and carried her dripping and laughing up to the stands, where waited his duffel bag filled with a tumble of work clothes and oranges from a Mildura orchard. How long since anybody called her Kid?

She allows herself more—*wallowing*, Jack would call it, but it's really too bright, too lovely to be called that, or to turn away from. The clean shock of ocean water that rippled through her, fingertips first, as she dove from the white concrete starters' block. No *ah-ahhh*ing about the cold, no time to waste. Gliding an inch below the surface, fifty yards on a single breath, the day's warmth beating down through the water. Playing knick-knack on her spine as the sun hauled itself higher. Knowing by something like instinct, something like sonar, where to turn; wheeling around and feeling her toes connect and flex against stony poolside; gulping in a lungful of air for the return lap.

The swimsuits she'd owned then: she could chart the whole decade on them. A new one every year, just about: '66, the lemon-butter yellow with pink flamingos at the hips; '67, the emerald-green two-piece with the starry thread running through; '68, the sophisticated navy-blue Jantzen with its white piping and keyhole. That one she wouldn't change even when the fashion did, she loved it so much. From age eighteen to twenty she wore it, flinging herself into the captive rectangle of ocean until finally the elastic disintegrated and the suit slumped around her brown thighs.

Once, a stingray washed into the pool overnight. It must have ridden a king tide across the barrier that partitioned the baths from the open sea, and she'd dived right in before seeing it. As she glissed across the forty-yard line, it was suddenly there beneath her, down on the floor of the pool, quietly lifting its edges like an egg in a pan. Evelyn doubled back over it and floated there awhile, staring down through the nine feet of water to where it rested, immense and blue-granite colored, with a constellation of white speckles. And its wings—was it right to call them wings? She didn't know—had the span of a Chinese kite.

How long did she hang there above it, imagining herself a silent aircraft hovering over an uncharted islet? She waited for the ray to do something, but it seemed either content enough or else resigned to a new life of enclosure. Maybe it felt safe there.

Though when she came back the next morning, it had choofed off, or been forcibly removed.

Nothing quite like that will ever happen again, she's sure— not now, not here. How could it? This long-reaching emptiness, grabbing right into you; nothing beautiful or unlikely could sneak up on you here. You'd see it coming, kicking up dust from miles away, and by the time it got here, it would already look spent, secondhand. Only the cruelty is astonishing, only the toxic boredom twisting imaginations just as the wind twists the cypress. The sight of Belle, strewn through the yard . . . She shivers.

Before Jack, she'd believed she would always live on the coast, at the lacy green edge of things. Was that so much to want? Evelyn feels dried-out here, older than her forty years. The last time she saw a stingray, it was something dreadful, a grotesque little flaunt of exoticism. A woman at the post office carrying a souvenir handbag from Thailand, the ray's skin dried to hard leather. The white diamond-shaped cluster of tiny bony pearls where the dorsal fin would be. Had been. Fitting, she thinks now, though the irony escaped her at the time.

It's very unique, she'd said to the woman, and the woman— orchestrator of fund-raisers for the PTA, CFA, ETC.; Ev couldn't re-member her name—smiled back at her with something like pity.

Well, a thing's either unique or it isn't, she'd said back over her shoulder, then moved up to the counter to collect her package.

The garage door goes up with a bit of a struggle, a bit of a screech. It's neater in there than it was this morning, Tetch having wrought a rough sort of order on the chaos. That was in keeping with the natural law of things; Jack busted things up, and his brother fixed them. Like a European folktale, something with ravens and black forests and woodsmen.

Clever with his hands, Tetch. What's left of them. Does she think about them, his hands, what they would be like? Sometimes. Just curiously. Well, anyone would. She's never known him to have a woman, but she supposes there must be some things the man keeps to himself in that warren of broken radios and hurt birds and obsolete encyclopedias. Maybe an awful lot, even in this town. Maybe especially in this town.

Watching him lope across the lawn this morning, the solemn poise about him. She might call it grace. Where to trace it?

Your father, was he more like you or more like . . . she'd once started to ask Jack, before thinking better of it. There was no telling. There was never any telling, besides the look he got sometimes. The slight twitch at the side of his mouth. His palms pressed down flat upon the tabletop. As if he could feel something trembling there in the wood, the way you might lay your hand to a rail line to know whether a train was coming. Or measure the distance of an oncoming storm by the seconds between the thunder and the lightning (or was it the other way around?).

He'd cock his head as if listening. It chilled her. She could never hear a thing.

Tetch (*Les*, she reminds herself, *Les*) seems fashioned of different stuff. Well, he is, really. A different mother—a fling, she must've been—who went and got herself shut away over some display of hysterics. Accidentally on purpose running the car off the road outside Inverloch, Les just a tiny thing strapped into the back. He turned up on a school night, as Jack told it, with the clothes he was wearing and half a bag of Twisties the careworker had bought for him. *All he could say was sorry, sorry, sorry.* Six years old, only a few months younger than Jack, but pond-eyed and nervy. Flinching at his half brother's feints. Hence Tetch, Tetchy, and the name had stuck to him like a bindi-eye. Even now, grown wiry and stoic and lantern-jawed. Jackal-jawed, says her sister, Estelle, who's sure that whatever is rotten in Jack must likewise be rotten in his brother, just more cunningly hidden.

They're not the same people, Stell.

Who ever said they were? I worry, though. You let him around those girls . . .

Oh, please.

Well, you never . . . Don't go telling me he's sound, though, love. Don't tell me there aren't a few loose wires up there.

And Evelyn does have to wonder sometimes: Are they some kind of unaccomplishable task? Herself and Jack and the girls? Not so much more than a giant clock or radio, a machine so big and broken he might spend his whole life tinkering away at it and never get to the part where he has to name a price. Why else?

She hoists the final box of decorations onto a newly cleared shelf, pushing it back flush against the wall, as far from sight as possible. Till next Christmas, and whatever that might drag with it.

Around her the useless clutter of the last several years. Somehow never enough money, but still too much stuff. Too much of the wrong stuff. The blue Jantzen swimsuit, she wishes she'd held on to that. Not to actually wear—snowball's chance she'd get into it now anyway; that body is long gone—but because it stood for something. For a *when.* What to call it, the *when*—her life before Jack? *Before I met your father.* The Coastal Years. Or she might call them the Prewar Years. *When you could put your hands like this*. Of course the war had been going on somewhere (well, she knew *where*) the entire time she'd been lapping the ocean baths, stringing those lazy summers end to end, sea-glass beads clacking onto an invisible length of fishing line. And some of the boys from that time, friends' boyfriends and older brothers, had been wrenched away to fight in it. There were debates in the papers, when she cared to look, speeches on TV and radio. The protests, the marches down Broadway, the moratoriums would all come later. But in any case it had sweet little to do with her, the notion of it as far away as the land it was being fought on.

It was still going on when she met Jack, but his time in it was done. You could believe that, looking at him then. He'd laugh at any old thing. At the smallest, stupidest … And his hair brilled up like Marlon Brando's, spilling over the right side of his forehead in dark, glossy waves, with the skew of his grin doing its best to balance that out, always lifting up higher at the left. That was how she first noticed him noticing her. Just standing there at the foot of the narrow stairway leading up to the projectionist's booth, gripping the bulky hexagonal canisters that housed the film she and Stell were waiting in line to see. What was it, even, that film? January in Melbourne, and the two of them were on loan to their aunt and uncle. Three whole weeks—what was there to do after walking a million laps of the Tan and trying to be polite about the oily jellyfish bath that was Port Phillip Bay? It was as hot as chip fat, and no nice place to swim, unless you took a car. The girls saw films. Anything and everything showing. That particular day it might have been that stupid vampire blockbuster Stella had been tugging her sleeve about. And when they'd gone to the candy bar for a couple of Cokes, there was the projectionist again, his smile skewiff, Bring us back a Cherry Ripe, love?

And why the hell not, she'd thought, just to see what it was like up there (airless, acrid, panic-causing; how could he have stood it? she'd later wonder, knowing what she came to know). But if she were honest—telling Stell to go on in and save her a seat, twirling the red-foiled chocolate bar like a baton—it was to see that slow curl of his smile.

Oh, come on, get off it, Stell said later. It wasn't a smile, you dolt, it was a bloody *leer.*

But for those first few years. When he could still stand things, or at least pretend to. When he could still stand to be around people. Before all the shrapnel had worked its way to the surface. *I wanna see you in uniform.* And she had wanted to. She'd been idiot enough to want that.

The last of the Coastal Years belonged to a burnt-orange halter bikini—part payment for a small-change fashion shoot she'd done at twenty, modeling a now-extinct line of beachwear while smoking a now-extinct brand of cigarette. Everything was burnt orange in those days. The '70s could really only be remembered in those saturated tangerines and iridescent blues. Even dreams played out in Kodachrome. Kids could be forgiven for believing the world truly looked like that then.

She'd been wearing the burnt orange on that last morning at the baths, when Jack came to scoop her out of the water; *This is it, Kiddo.* And an hour later her hair was dried to pale, stiff waves, to salty blond meringue as she packed the car with whatever would fit into it, her father standing tall and stock still on the veranda.

Is this how you're thanking us? He was booming up there, at first, but he quickly fell soft when he saw there would be no stopping her. We didn't buy you that car so you could drive it away on us, love. Your mother and I . . .

But her mother was inside, refusing to play a part in the drama. Refusing to look or to speak whenever Ev went in for another armload of dresses. This was the same tactic she'd employed with Ev and Stell when they were tantruming children. Eyes on the road. Let them exhaust themselves of their nonsense. Now she just stood there in the kitchen, rinsing and re-rinsing the dishcloth, wringing it out tight, wiping down the draining board. Stell had already left for school, and so missed the opportunity to be corrupted by the scene.

That afternoon, Evelyn had driven as far as Yass, and there Jack took over. That Janis Joplin song on the radio every couple hundred ks and Evelyn la-da-da-la-na-nahing along, tuning out the lyrics that didn't suit her, any words that didn't fit the thrill of flight, of freedom freedom freedom, and they reached Wangaratta by dark. That motel with its faded apricot carpet and stuccoed walls, where even the fake plants looked thirsty, and they'd fucked in a bed for the first time. Thin sheets and thinner walls, light from the hallway cigarette machine creeping under the doorsill. She didn't care. It was trashy as all get-out, but she was reveling in it. After those few times in Melbourne—shaking sand out of her clothes, or sneaking up to Jack in the bio box, or standing with her back against the Brighton breakwall, him pulling from her at the last possible second and turning to the ocean, pumping his cock toward the spray—after all that, this sagging motel bed felt *real*. (Though much later, she'd catch herself missing, oddly, those hasty, claustrophobic tussles in the bio box, the tattoo of film ricketing off the reel and the sound it made matching up to the stammering pulse of blood behind her eyelids, her hands greasy with his hair, and the theater downstairs erupting over something Newman or McQueen had either won or escaped from.)

In the motel, she lay on top of the covers, and it felt salacious, indulgent, like they were trying on the lives of other people. Go ahead and scream if you want, sweetheart, Jack had told her. We're never going to see any of these bastards again.

Lani was born shaking into her arms in the middle of that decade, and she would not stop shaking until the beginning of the '80s. Evelyn tries to remember this shaking whenever she runs into the rangy, foulmouthed creature who haunts the room at the end of the hallway, shut in there with the throb of something dreary. Tries to remember the trembling of the little spine felt through terry-toweling jumpsuits, the vulnerable blossom mouth. She stares at the poster tacked up and torn at the corner nearest the doorknob; the band members look like they're all dying of the same disease. Behind the poster, Lani's door is all splinters and strips of packing tape. Evelyn knocks and waits before trying the handle, knowing it'll be locked whether her oldest daughter is in there or not. No energy for a row this afternoon; she just follows the routine disarmament the two of them have fallen into over the last few years. These shitty locks; they're mostly cosmetic anyway. Won't really keep anyone out, will just slow them down long enough so that whoever's on the other side has time to get their pants up. She worries at the snib with a butter knife, and Lani's door swings open on an empty room, gauzy curtains drawn back to reveal the flyscreen with its escape hatch sliced into one corner. Gone, then. Today and forever. Even when she comes back this afternoon, or tonight—tomorrow morning; who knows?—Evelyn will find no way of reaching her, no way of getting her to listen. Through threats or through fists, neither works now. Lately she's astonished herself with her own ferocity, how it closes over her, suffocates reason. How the marks on her daughter's body have begun to mirror her own. Lani that morning, reaching for a high spot with the paint scraper, and her pajama top hiking up to show a familiar purpling at the hip, door-handle height. Law of conservation. Absorption and emission. Ev tries to remember what she learned in fifth-form science. How it all has to go somewhere. How light becomes heat and heat becomes—what? The science teacher's hand spiraling to show the chain of elements. Very tall, he was, very Dutch. His name was . . . But it doesn't matter; she knows this isn't what he was on about when he set up those tabletop experiments of pulleys and weights.

She stands in the bedroom doorway, butter knife held loose at her side. New Year's Eve. (*Happy New Year's, Eve!*) There comes a point. There comes a point where you have to say, Here it is. Here is what life looks like. Where you stop turning your head away, cupping your ears—*la-da-da-la-na-nah*—because you finally understand it won't do any good.

For years now, she's been waking to the same knowledge: This is not my life. Gray eucalypts shaking out there in the stonewashed sky and Jack's loose copper change scattered across the veneer bedside table. No, none of this is right. None of this fits. There's been some hash-up. Someone else out there living her real life, running up the mileage on it the way you would a stolen car. But they'll own up eventually. They'll have to, with all the guilt and the worry wearing them down. The joyride can't go on forever.

She'd seen it so clearly. This whole time, all these years, she could just about smell it—a salt breeze playing curtains into that bright, high-ceilinged room.

But this is it. The butter knife, the torn flysceen, the cluster of dorsal pearls on someone else's souvenir handbag. This familiar taste in her mouth, like colloidal silver, which she understands and refuses to understand.

Outside, tires churn the sparse gravel of the driveway. Estelle. Out of the blue, as always, as if to catch her out at something. Down the dark hallway goes Evelyn, past the sunsets and gorges and waterfalls tacked over fist-pocked plasterboard. The Kakadu gorge is her favorite of these, a big hole hiding a small hole; she knows no one else who would find this funny. For Christmas she'd thought of buying Jack a stud finder. As if to say *Punch here*. But it seemed a lot of effort to go to just to humiliate someone. Or more likely enrage them. And it turned out he wouldn't have been there to unwrap it anyway; the shirt she'd bought instead is still tucked down in the bottom of the wardrobe.

The mottled shape of her sister appears at the sidelight, hullooing and drumming lurid orange fingernails against the glass.

Evvie? Home?

She opens the door. Stella in pale crepe de chine, looking like the heat wouldn't dream of wilting her. That false light in her eyes and a high arc of brow at the butter knife still dangling from Ev's fingers.

Oh, my love . . . It'll take more than that to chase me off.

Come on, Evelyn says, already half turning. Come on in out of that heat.

Her sister's face sometimes. When she comes into the house and takes in the dirty lino, the dishes stacked up in the sink, or any fresh violence wreaked in one of Jack's storms. Ev doesn't want to see her seeing it, the judgment she'll find there. She walks ahead, giving Stell a few moments to compose the neat diamond of her face. But by the time they reach the kitchen, she still hasn't quite managed it, so Evelyn turns away again, quickly, running the tap into the kettle.

At certain safe distances, they are good friends. When there are a couple hundred kilometers of Hume and a decent stretch of Melbourne between them, her sister is the best person she knows. But up close, sharing air . . . It's this house that does it, makes the two of them strangers. Perched on the fridge, the card Stell posted two weeks ago: *It Is Better to Have Loved and Lost . . .* above an illustration of an elegant woman shrugging, gloriously flippant. The easy, stupid humor of other people.

Stell moves a stack of newspapers from one of the dining chairs, then sits and lights an Alpine, flicking her eyes around for Jack's abalone-shell ashtray, which has been emptied, washed, and—for the first time in its post-mollusk history—put away. Evelyn retrieves it from the cupboard and clacks it down in front of Stell, who taps her ash and says, wide-eyed, So! He really is gone for good then?

With her shoulders Evelyn answers, Who knows? But she's thinking, If he is gone for good. If he's gone for good, then maybe she doesn't have to tell him. Doesn't have to tell anyone. Is *exempt* from telling. Would he want to hear it anyway? Hardly. Would he say, *Look, we're keeping it,* and come running right back? Hardly. And what if he did, and what—oh god—if it turned out to be a boy. He'd be harder on a boy, she knows it. The one she'd lost had been a boy. Too early to tell, *conclusively,* but she just knew. With each of the girls she'd gotten sun spots, and that time there were none, even though it had been well into summer.

Gone for good. She tries to hold steady: the fist knuckled up and shaking under her chin. The near-constant throb of a door handle in the small of her back, the bruises that bloomed overnight, like Casa Blancas, and even she couldn't say where half of them came from.

And she looks at Stell on the other side of the kitchen, looking ten years younger instead of two. The taut, haughty structure of her face, and hair the color that Ev's had once been, until it started falling out, inexplicably, after Ruby was born. Hanks of it, in spite of the gentle pull of a wide-tooth comb, till there was nothing left. When it did come back, it came back white. Dandelion down, tic-toc fluff she imagined might blow away if the wind so chose. She wasn't yet thirty then. Now she pharmacy-dyes it herself to a pale honey. But somehow it always comes off looking brassy when she's next to Stell, as though they're standing in two different kinds of light, Evelyn always caught in the wrong kind.

She lays a hand over her stomach, wordlessly apologizing to the *something* gaining mass there. No, she can't. With or without him, she can't have this one.

She might tell Stell.

And Stell will say *You little idiot, Evvie. After everything. You still let him put it in you?*

No, she won't tell Stell, who is already bored, or uneasy anyway, just with being here. Moving bits of paper around on the table. Flipping through junk mail catalogs, the girls' school exercise books, anything to keep her hands busy. There's Ru's report on outer space. *Did you know . . .* And then the names of the moons of Mars.

Where're the girls today?

God only knows. If you can find them, you can keep them. Evelyn continues hunting through the dish rack for a cup that isn't grimy or hairlined with cracks. Was the drive okay?

The drive was fine. Don't happen to have anything stronger than tea?

Bad news?

No, no news. Only that it's . . . It couldn't hurt to celebrate a bit, could it?

Oh, right. Well, I think there's vodka back there somewhere, if Lani hasn't sniffed it out.

That'll do.

Or no, it was rum maybe. White rum. Will it work with cordial?

Whatever it is, is fine. Estelle rummages in her paper-straw bag, producing plastic tubs of sugarcoated almonds, macaroons like little crescent moons nestled close to one another. Leftovers from her event-planning work, someone else's Yarra Valley wedding. She snaps the lids off, as though to coax her nieces from hiding. As though they might come running in, meowing like cats do at the sound of a can opener.

The freezer is choked with ice, barricaded by captive packets of peas and beans, vegetable medleys. The rum, it'll take some excavating, Ev says.

Forget it. Tea's fine. And Ev knows that it isn't, isn't fine at all, but she closes the freezer door and resumes her search for passable china.

Whenever she visits, her sister brings word of their parents. Dispatches, Ev thinks, because Stell knows better than to tell too much, to throw light into the gulf that separates their lives from hers. But she knows enough. She knows their father can manage stairs again after cracking a hip in the least heroic of ways—not falling in the lunge pen but slipping in the shower, like an old man, though he isn't one, really, not yet. Not far past sixty. (She had the girls write him a card, a get-well-soon, but if it got a response, she never heard about it.) She knows, too, that their mother has finally won her twelve-year campaign to move permanently upcoast to the country place; that they'd be shifting everything there after the summer rolled out of the way.

Also through Stell: cards and small gifts for Ruby and Lani. Trinkets for the kind of girls their grandparents hoped they were or might be. Never money. They didn't trust Ev, after the Corvette.

Evelyn worries over the sort of news running back across the wire. What is broken. What is missing, presumed hocked. The state of the house. How wild the girls are. How tall the grass, how ice-locked the freezer. And so the cups. The cups, at least.

She places a mug—unremarkable, save that it is undamaged—in front of her sister, whose fingernails immediately go to work on the tea tag. Sit down, will you please? You make me jumpy when you're hovering.

Evelyn sits, with paring knife and a sweet backyard lemon, cutting wedges and arranging them around a saucer to cover the fact of there being no milk.

Estelle stares at her. You look better, you know.

Do I? Knowing better than to ask *Better than when?*

I'd say. It's always the same thing, when he leaves. You look absolutely harrowed for the first little while. As though he's managed to belt you up from the inside as well. But after he's been gone a few weeks . . .

She leans in close then, holding her smoke, scrutinizing. Reading Ev's eyes, as though trying to peer through to some secret lacuna. Finally she sits back, satisfied.

It's like the lights come back on, she says.

Evelyn feels an urge to bite into one of the lemon wedges, to feel the bright rush in her mouth, cutting through the unwelcome metallic taste. She does so, peeling the yellow strip of rind away from her teeth, but if Stell thinks this odd, she doesn't let it show.

The lights come back on, Stell says, again. And when they do, I think, Ah, this time she'll wake up. Maybe this time. You know, there was a while—okay, truth be told, it was years. For years after you left. I'd go into your room and I'd go through everything, just because I could, just because you weren't there to get miffed about it. Your books, even. I read *The Living and the Dead* two years early, out of spite.

That's a pretty industrious kind of spite; I never finished a page of that. Evelyn pushes the lemon plate forward. I thought we were okay friends, back then.

Stell gives her a look. So did I. But you never even called. Anyway. I came around to realizing that whatever was still in your room was only there because you hadn't wanted it. None of it mattered to you, or not badly, anyway.

I wrote. And it was only things, says Evelyn, not believing herself for an instant and probably not sounding like it.

My point, though—*I* knew that. *I* knew none of it mattered. But for Mum it was like you'd died or something. The way people get funny when kids die? It stayed like a fucking Evelyn shrine in there. It was only a few years ago that Mum decided, enough! Enough's enough, and—

Stell blows smoke at the ceiling, then sends her words up there after it. Look, if he's gone for good— If he's really gone for good, then why don't you?

Why don't I what?

Oh, don't be thick. Don't pretend to be, she hisses, grinding her cigarette into the shell's iridescent hollow. They'll help, if it means getting the girls out of this . . .

Out of this what?

This. Situation.

Situation?

I'm not saying. Jesus, don't twist my words, will you? I'm just saying it's an option. You do have options.

God, you've always been on their side.

But Stell says she's on no one's side. I'm Switzerland, she says from the other side of the table.

Ev shakes her head. No. I'm not crawling back, end of story.

Though sometimes she doesn't even have to close her eyes and she's there. On that gate, hitching a leg over. Breathing air that smells of lucerne and sun-cracked leather. There's the off-the-track mare who trusts her so completely she doesn't even need a bridle, doesn't even need to saddle her. Ev can just throw a blanket over her broad back and guide her by the flimsiest of ropes, the gentlest of tugging at the tough old mouth. Could almost guide her by thought alone, thisaway thisaway, down to the wide tannin river and right out into the middle, the mare wet to her flanks and the current sucking sweetly around Evelyn's ankles.

It's all still going on up there—the country place—her father's horses still velvet-nosing his shoulder, and her mother going straw-hatted and cork-heeled to the Sunday race meets.

On wet, moony nights eels still migrate from dam to river, rippling through the sodden grass in gray droves, biblical. Yearlings still breeze circles round the lunge pen, Aemon turning them into bankers, spinning them into dusty gold.

A horse is a stupid animal when it comes right down to it. That was Aemon, his denim philosophizing as she watched him long-reining a blue roan.

A horse'll run itself to death, eat itself to death, drink itself to death if you let it. It's the only animal that needs to be learnt restraint.

Evelyn still doesn't know if this is a true thing, or just idle talk, or idle talk with something edifying woven into it, idle talk she was meant to heed.

But that roan. His coloring almost birdlike. Blue Boy there in the near dark, Aemon pivoting with him; Ironbark when he raced. And after him came Old Pardon, Kiley's Run, Wind's Message—their father named all his horses after Banjo Paterson poems, bush ballads, convinced that the spirit of the gentleman gambler came down and touched their fetlocks, brought luck. Whether it was luck or whether it was Aemon, they could move, all right, could earn.

There were afternoons, huge and aimless, when no one else was in the house; no Jack, no girls. Just Evelyn sitting on the back steps with the paper, weekend supplements in loose sheaves sifting all around her, held down against the breeze by a coffee mug or sandwich plate. The race form across her knees as she scanned for names she might recognize. It was only the once she went so far as to take herself into town to place a meek each-way bet on Come-By-Chance. (*No location was assigned it, not a thing to help one find it;* she'd always liked that one herself, remembering the messmate burr of her father's voice reading it.) Standing there in the fug of the TAB while leery dropkicks with nicotine beards watched her watching the screens. The colt was third-to-favorite, and he came in right where he was expected to, and Evelyn made her money back to the dollar. She felt like breaking something. Like laughing and like breaking something in the same instant. But she went quietly to the window and ran the ticket through, collecting the few dollars that were neither losings nor takings—or both at the same time— and spent them on a bottle of sweet cider along with a doughy éclair from the chain bakery. Both were sweating by the time she got them home to sit again on the back steps, licking slicks of melted icing from her fingers and chasing it down with starry mouthfuls of cider as Belle wriggled out from under the lantana, her fur festooned with cobwebs and blossoms. Evelyn tore off bits of the pastry and tossed them up for the collie to catch, wondering when life had become defined by lack. When had it started taking its shape from the things that were no longer in it?

And now here's Stell—on whose orders, exactly?—still waiting for an answer as though she hasn't already had one.

Look, Stell says. What is it you actually want?

But Evelyn can't say. She wants, badly . . . There's no way of putting it. It's all back there somewhere, behind her. Irretrievable. She wants for the burnt-orange beginning. The Jantzen. The Corvette. Those *things*. But there's no vehicle can get her back to it, she knows that. And there are public places where she wants to scream *Help!* Where she might've even mouthed it once: *Somebody, please.* Pulling a bread bag down from a wire rack at the supermarket. But there's never anybody.

They never forgave me, about that bloody car. And it *was* just a car, after all. After that, all they ever gave me was ultimatums.

You'll put a crick in your neck, my love, looking back like that.

Right. Lot's wife. What was her name, even? Did she even get a name?

Estelle shakes her head. No. Or if she did, well, I don't remember it. They never told us.

Evelyn almost tells, then. About the child. Almost asks, *What should I . . .* But, as if to preempt that horror, Stell scrapes her chair back and says, Anyway. I'm sick to death of running over this same old mucky ground. You're going to do what you're going to do, and the rest of us will just have to—

She pulls herself up then, sudden. Goes so far as to cover her mouth. Sorry, she says. Evvie. We do love you, you know?

Evelyn nods, but there's something about the way Estelle's said it, leaning so heavy on the word *do*, that makes Evelyn want her gone.

And soon enough, she is. Going, slinging her bag off the back of the chair and onto the crook of her slender arm, clamping a hand down over her cigarette packet, leaving the biscuits to go soft on the table. Creasing her eyes up in a way that looks like smiling, almost. And Evelyn venturing an arm around her in a way that is an embrace, almost, feeling her ribs there beneath the creamy silk.

Next time.

Next time.

Almost. From the shade of the doorway she watches her sister back that zippy little Japanese number down the drive, hand fluttering out the window and a beep for goodbye. *Back to Yuppieland.* Jack's voice there, in her head—he's poisoned everything.

•

It was meant to be a start-afresh, this place. A way of bricking over the squalor and damp of their early unsettled years together, when they'd jumped from house to house, running out on the rent once or twice when they had to. Or when it seemed fair to. The roachy one-bedroom flat in Collingwood; the carved-up St. Kilda mansion, where syringes sprang up in the garden like weeds; the dilapidated bungalow that backed onto the railway line in Fairfield. But she figures them happiest in that ramshackle weatherboard, with its moaning hot-water system, its peeling linoleum. Suspicious spills on the carpet—they'd laid their mattress over these and he'd used his rough hands to massage baby oil into her swelling belly, into her achy back and feet, aching himself from concreting jobs and shelf-stacking jobs and night watchman jobs, from dawn shifts and swing shifts and long overnights. And it wasn't the coast, but there was water, close enough that she could walk there. Or waddle there, after a fashion. Spread his old coat on the riverbank and doze there like a cat, belly pointed toward the late-summer sun. Once waking up to find him standing over her, watching her snooze.

Reckoned I might find you here.

She'd sat up, sleep-sozzled. You're off early. Tell me they didn't . . .

Yep. The arse again. Here's your hat, hey, what's your hurry?

And still, that time was best. It wasn't till later—toward the end of that year, or the beginning of the next—that he got rough. It might've started when he was loving her. His forearm across her collarbone, pinning her down. Thumbs working deep into her thigh flesh. With her lying there thinking that'll bruise, that'll bruise. Sometimes he played it like a game. Sometimes not. Letting her lift herself a little way from the mattress, only so far, then pushing her back down to it. Just like the way he spoke to her sometimes—talking her up and then knocking her back, flattening her.

God, you're beautiful. You're so fucking . . . when you wear your hair like that. Do other men like that? Those other men you screw around with? Do they like it when you wear your hair like that?

And he hadn't believed, she couldn't get him to believe, at first, that Lani was his. He wanted proof.

Proof? Well, you could frigging look at her.

I could look at her if she could shut the fuck up for a second.

When Lani was a tiny thing, Evelyn used to bundle her into the Corvette and just drive around. Anywhere. Any old where, in any direction. She'd had to, those early years, with all the trembling and the squall—Lani howling like the earth itself splitting open, and there was not a thing to calm her but to carry her shaking and tear-soaked out to the car. She'd lull right down then, being strapped into her carrier on the passenger side, and by the end of the street she'd be still. Then when Ru came along, she was a sturdier creature, but of course she too, she'd come along too, making big eyes from the carrier as Evelyn did her best not to get pulled over with Lani sitting propped up behind the wheel. Her sleepy child-weight against Evelyn's body was like a kind of blessing, the seat belt encircling both of them, safe enough.

She'd drive until both girls slept, and sometimes longer, however far she could get on half of what was in the tank—god that thing just drank fuel—until the petrol gauge told her: *Home now.* And even then. She'd had to will her foot down on the brake. Because everything held and breathing in that small space was her own. Hers alone, it felt. And she'd thought about it. Whether or not Jack was back there at the house, sleeping off some poison, or disappeared again, or checked back into the repat, tranqued out with neuroleptics and hobbycrafts, a different kind of stranger to her. She had thought about it. Ru dozing in the bassinet there, and her oldest curled against her, not seeming to mind or to wake at the jostle of knees when Evelyn switched between gears. Maybe twenty dollars in her purse and somehow a week until pension, but if she left her ring and, fine, her watch too, as collateral—she'd done all that before—that might get her a full tank of petrol, which would get them as far as . . . where? Not far enough. Not the full night of hours it would take to get in sight of her parents' white bullnose veranda. But if she could. With the girls like limp, sleepy kittens from the long trip. They wouldn't be able to tell her—even if she didn't say she was sorry—wouldn't be able to tell her no.

But she could never quite bring herself to do it. Run out on him like that. And it was never as simple as money. It was never as simple as pride, because she's not sure she's ever had much of that either. Or if she does, it hasn't turned out to be worth much, not when it comes right down to it.

Something else, then. When he'd brought Belle home, rescued her, you could see it. The good that was there. She could wait it out, she'd thought. The war in him. She could lie there beside him while he dreamed that whole mess backwards, thrashing out as he sometimes would, as he sometimes needed to. Step for step, just walk backwards through the rubber trees and come out the nearer side, the way he'd gone in.

She'd thought of it like that—imagined it as being something like diving into water from a great height. You just had to make sure the water was as deep as the fall, or else you were cooked. A wheelchair case. He was still resurfacing. He'd come up eventually; she'd always believed so. Come up gasping, and she'd be there.

So always, in the end, she'd pull over to the shoulder. Sit there listening to the engine tick, the sleep-breathing of her daughters. Their daughters. The car buffeted now and again by road trains. And then she'd turn around.

The screen door lattices the backyard into shards, into a weary mosaic. She had once loved the magnolia, but passing it now, she turns her head away. Clamps shut her eyelids at the memory of Belle, or what was left of her, and of Jack's face afterward, more harrowed than ever. And also—though it belonged to a different afternoon; spring, it must've been, the magnolia dropping its fleshy petals into the grass—the memory of spitting bloody drool, twisting a loosened tooth from its socket while he watched her from the back doorway, both of them numb to it, awed even, the space between them seemingly made solid, impassable. Then him coming down the stairs with a clean tea towel wrapped around a bag of frozen peas, as though the violence were not his own work. She'd stood out here with the cold bundle pressed to her face, already feeling the swell, her premolar cupped in her palm. She closed her fingers around it and shook it in her fist like a die, then flung it into the magnolia's dark, glossy leaves, the way you'd make a wish. The way a person might make a wish if they knew what in the hell to wish for.

She's walking there before she knows she is, to Les, taking the back route, the tramped-down path that skirts paddocks and the backs of houses. Along the fence line, some animal reek. Tufts of brindle fur snagged along the barbwire. Leftovers from where boys had strung up the remnants of fox and rabbit carcasses.

Bait, Lani had explained to her, matter-of-fact.

Bait?

Panther bait.

Oh, come off it . . .

Her daughter had only shrugged. Not meeting her eye, dark lines etched into her lips from a gruesome shade of lipstick she'd been made to wipe away.

She finds her brother-in-law at work on something—always something—dismantled electrical guts spilling over yesterday's newspaper. A radio, unshelled, that he shifts off the table.

Whose's that?

No one's yet. Take your fancy?

Before they moved here. When they were just visiting. The first time she'd met Les—though he'd been introduced to her right away, from the get-go, as Tetch—he'd poured her tea into an eggshell-frail cup, placed it in her hands as if it were alive. And she'd let herself get swallowed up, ballooning belly and all, in the big cord-upholstered armchair in the living room, thinking, Okay, this will do. Something like this . . . she could stomach it. The big windows and his veggie patch and the bookshelves lined with outdated leather-bound *Britannicas* that had never heard of Maggie Thatcher. And then by some magic the house had come up, within spitting distance. Dog's will, Les had called it, that odd, shaggy humor of his.

What's changed since then? Some things plenty, though here, in Les's kitchen, hardly anything at all. Only that of late, her brother-in-law has a way of looking at her. Clear and piercing. Not unkindly. More than kindly, if she's honest. And it's harmless, she's sure, but loud as a spoken word. Which word, exactly, she doesn't know. Alone with him, she needs small, useless things to do with her hands: the fingering of a skirt hem, the turning up and rolling down of a sleeve. Needs places to look that are not him, his gray-blue eyes. Her gaze flicking around the small kitchen (Weet-Bix box, souvenir plate from Broome . . .) as though her whole body might be stammering its response to a question she's not even sure she's heard right. When all either of them can manage to say aloud is:

Cuppa?

No, thanks all the same.

Something cool, then?

Really. She feels a thirst, but asking for anything, accepting anything now seems treacherous.

He places a stumpy bottle of ginger beer in front of her and says, Well it's there looking at you anyway.

Oh. Ta. She uncaps the drink, listens to it hiss at her.

He's waiting for it, she sees. Whatever it is. There are his hands, resting neat upon the table. The barely interrupted span between the thumb and middle finger. She takes a swallow so she doesn't have to speak yet.

Hit the spot? His clear eyes, the harsh weather of his skin. Heat always close to the surface, a few days' pale stubble coming in around his lean jaw.

She feels a sharp, clean panic and looks at her own hands. Sees how high the veins are running, how dark, standing out from her still-thin wrists. She feels betrayed by her body, by her blood. Thinks, Who wants to be seen clearly? Who wants that so late into things?

I figure you'd tell me, but— Well. I know there's loyalty and all that. So I thought I better just ask. But you haven't, have you? Heard anything?

He regards her a moment. From Jack? You don't think I'd tell you?

Well, loyalty and all that. Sorry, I shouldn't have even. Shouldn't have asked. She swigs from the ginger beer.

I would tell you, he says. She sees his jaw working on nothing and tries to tell if he's lying to her, then decides she doesn't care. Or that she does care, but it doesn't matter.

The truck is out there in the drive. Reliable. She could manage it. And absolutely, he'd lend it to her, no question. She realizes with little wonder that he'd probably give her anything she asked, anything he had. What to do with that? There isn't a thing in the world to do with that.

She could find Jack herself, without too much detective work. A single morning in St. Kilda, maybe Collingwood. That's all it would take. A bit of door knocking, asking around the sleazy soakholes with the rusted-on types who'd call her *girlie* and *darling*, thinking that what she was after was to feel young. She could track him down, could probably shame him home. Bring his rough hand to her belly, tell him, *This time.* But no.

A horse'll run itself to death. A useless fact, if it was one. Well, frigging let it, then.

Thank you, she says. For the drink. Pushing her chair away from the table, handing him back the half-empty bottle. Seeing herself as Les must: a bratty child who has what she came for. She tries to fix it, babbles moronically about her dad's crystal set, knowing she's only making things worse.

She walks home the long way, along the roadside, across front yards when they appear. Parked cars crowding drives, barbecue smoke lifting into the cooling air.

Before it gets to twilight, before fox o'clock, she sees to the rabbits, to getting them fed and shut away safe. Last year's birthday present from Stell.

You could breed them if you wanted to, was Stell's reasoning. Sell them to people at the girls' schools, in the *Trading Post*. Earn a little something for yourself. They're pricey bunnies, let me tell you.

An-fucking-gora, more mouths to feed. Jack again.

But they don't need so much, really. Mostly she just pulls up fistfuls of thistles from around the forty-gallon drum of rusty rainwater, likes to watch their grass-stained mouths work at grinding it away, pulling it all in like ticker tape. Simple little clockwork creatures.

She brushes her fingers through their long, silky fur, trying to comb out the tangles and burrs while they're distracted with their eating. They don't like that, though, try to shimmy away from her hands, her fingers still sticky with thistle milk.

I should just shave the two of you, she murmurs. I should knit jumpers out of you little dolts. That'd be something.

III
Breakwall

FIRST LIGHT, EARLY DECEMBER. WARM SUMMER STORM AND NO smokes. Three sleeps till pension day. Drove the wet black Hume right down to Melbourne. Looking for tobacco, found her big sunglasses in the glove box. Nothing for her to hide now anyway.

Take take take.

Parked in a leafy side street, one of the rich suburbs. Sat there waiting for the shakes to let up, listening to rain on the roof. Remember that was comforting once. The sound of rain, the smell of it. A long time ago.

Ten days sleeping in the car. Shaving in the servo, buying McDonald's coffee just to use the shitter, till a room opened up at the Regal. Real smart-arse on the stairwell said the last bugger topped himself. Found last bugger's lighter behind the chest of drawers. A girl in a red bikini, but when you go to light a smoke, her togs disappear. Very classy.

In case there is any misunderstanding, I think I should say, sir, that we decided in principle some time ago—weeks and weeks ago—that we would be willing to do this . . .

Pay phone on Grey Street. Could call her. Say *Happy Christmas, darling.* Then what?

Waking with a palmful of cigarette burns. Not sure how they got there. Or even who put them there. A well-loved copy of *Playboy* left under the mattress. The centerfolds getting too scrawny. Like little girls. Sick.

Thinking of maybe looking up Foxy. Thinking of maybe getting a hit, but who in their right mind trusts the stuff these days. Cut with glass and milk sugar and Christ knows.

No place to be alone here. No way to get away from the people and the sound of St. Kilda throwing up on itself. Front bar of the Esplanade like a tin of shit-faced sardines. Beach not much better. Idiots splashing naked into the grotty water. At your own peril, arseholes. Stood a while on the pier, feeling old— forty-fucken'-four, is all—then lit out for Brighton. Ten klicks on and ten years back to where she's standing on the breakwater. Not so far away, either way of looking at it. Not too far.

When you think of happiness, what picture do you have in your mind?

A chopper flying over. Sure, that'll do it. Channel Seven chopper, and all the rest. Car backfiring in the street. But also the smallest, friendliest things. Silver thermos like an artillery shell.

Certain smells. Ev rubbing Tiger Balm into Ruby's achy little back. That'll do it. Sunsets and sunrises, a particular color in the sky. That right there is what war does. Takes a tire iron to beauty. To the smallest, friendliest things.

What was there before? Walking the dam wall at Maroondah. Jody holding her damp hair up off her sweaty neck. A scruffy white dog running after a car. Race days and sprinklers turning lazy circles. Road-tripping all the way up to Broken Bay to see Pat and Maile in oyster season, and the big moon hanging huge and leery above the Hawkesbury. *Rabbit moon*, said Jody, standing on the dock and pointing out the ears and paws. Her long, pearly arm outstretched. Telling the story of how he jumped straight into the fire to cook his own scrawny self for a poor man's dinner. Girl knew some strange stuff. Somewhere out there, people are still living these things. Backyard cricket. Little cubes of cheese speared on toothpicks. All at the wrong end of a telescope. So small it could be covered with a hand.

Dear Sir, I am writing to inform you, in relation to your liability . . .

Only won the lotto once, and that was it. Happy birthday. Prize was a medical examination and a free trip on the Vung Tau Ferry.

The mess Tetch made of his hands. Didn't even bother to make it look like an accident.

Black leopard at the Pucka barracks. Sociable little bastard. Name meant "chief" in some Asian language. Or maybe it was Latin. Never was much chop with languages.

. . . that you are required, in accordance with the provisions of the National Service Act . . .

Kepala, that was him. General. Big boss. Even though he was only the size of a terrier when he was smuggled in. No one knew the first thing about panthers. Or black leopards—there a difference? Didn't matter. He grew burly on mess scraps, chicken carcasses. Cookie said he liked rat-pack beef best. His enclosure a cute little training project for the sappers. *Don't forget the spa bath, boys.*

Let me repeat, in simple terms, why we are in Vietnam.

Turned twenty-one propped up on a sandbag in a rubber plantation. *You too, hey?*

Yeah, and Foxy, said Wilson. *Trifecta.*

See these little pricks today with their caps turned wrong way round. Smart-mouthing outside the supermarket. Wanna give them a belting and a haircut and another belting.

Trifecta, all right. Hope whoever grabbed those marbles got himself a lotto ticket.
    Well I hope he got syphilis. Black syphilis.

One year. One stinking year out of forty-four, then a lifetime of four hours' sleep on a good night, waking to the same dark dread every morning, same lead in the belly. Life split in half, a neat whack with a hatchet, into the Before and the After. Good things still happened in the After, but it was like they were echoes. Shadows of things from the first two decades. Things that got ripped to rags trying to sneak across that one-year wire.

What're you waiting for, Burroughs? Written invitation? In you hop, boy-oh. That's where it started—Jackrabbit Burroughs, tunnel rat. Pisser. Remember going in. Wet webbing across the face, gut like a sack of live snakes. Don't remember climbing out. That poetry? What the head-quacks would say to that.

We are there because we believe in the right of people to be free.

Smell of hexamine. Dragging arse through the light green and someone singing "Blue Bayou." Miserable cunt.

Foxy asking, like an idiot, *What do y'reckon we're doing here?* That started them.
We're here, Foxy my darling, because Ho Chi Minh kicked over Mr. President's tricycle.

Boredom and rain. Some of the guys learned to whittle linking chains from dead branches or wood salvaged out of trashed villages. Foxy could get them up to a couple of feet. Just something to pass the time and pass the time . . . But it came to be a kind of code. *How is it today? Oh, it's a six-link day.* Meaning: *Here we all are in the sweet-fuck-all.*

. . . required, in accordance with the provisions of the National Service Act, to submit yourself to medical examination before a Medical Board . . .

In Queensland, Finch was studying marine science, but in Vietnam he studied coin and card and knife tricks. You name it, he'd mangle it. *Is this your card?* And 'course it never was. He'd be holding up a two of clubs when Papa Dickson had pulled a seven of spades.

We are there because we want peace, not war . . . doing his best Harold Holt.

Seppo jokes left over from World War Two. Hand-me-down humor. What do you get when you cross a . . . Where does a Yank keep his . . . Beer like sex in a canoe . . . How do ya separate two mating crocodiles?

Letters home lousy with white lies. Then big fibs. Then nothing.

Looked up one night, and there was that jackrabbit moon riding over the Song Dong Nai. So glad to see that little bastard. Should've guessed then; Dear Johned first mail after Balmoral. Not much to do about it. Have a few bottles of tiger piss and get defoliated.

We are there because we do not believe that our great Pacific partner, the United States, should stand alone for freedom.

Letters from home saying useless things, soft things. Remembered Tetch as a kid. Crying and pissing himself over a love tap. Just a love tap. How Mum shielded him, swaddled him up in cotton wool. And he wasn't even hers. And look at what good it did.

Our great Pacific partner? Jesus. Hope the bitch puts out.

Reed collapsed a burrow of baby mongooses while he was digging a shell scrape. Mamasan Mongoose off at mongoose work. One of the pups got cleaved in half by the entrenching tool, but Reed wrapped the other three up in his dirty singlet. *Hey, who wants some cobra repellent?*

Your Sense of Feeling. A feeling of irritation in the eyes, nose, or throat or on the skin is an urgent warning to protect yourself.

Protect yourself?

Smell of decay in everything, of wet, creeping rot. Creeping right into your guts.

Her initials still there, hidden under the black of the panther. J L dug in deep with an upholstery needle and colored with biro ink. The ghost of them showing through sometimes. Why only sometimes? Wondered what it meant. As if everything had to mean something.

Finch slicing himself with his balisong in the process of a double rollover. Foxy shaking his head, *If I was a crook dolphin, I'd cross my flippers and hope for a different fish doctor.*

Rikki, Tikki, and Tavi. Of course. Even the regs had read Kipling. Can't remember whose was which. One disappeared overnight. Another got sick after Wilson fed it stuff-all but powdered milk. It grew too weak to hold its sorry little rodent head up, and Wilson had to stomp on it. The only one that stuck it out was Reed's, tame enough to ride his shoulder. At night it would run around his hootchie snacking on beetles and wolfing up chomper ants. *Hey, Wilson. Betcha wish you'd shared ya camp pie.*

Reed had been a sign writer, would go on back to being a sign writer once he got home to the Great Back There. But during that shitful year he sketched portraits on the gold paper from cigarette packets. On wrappers from rat packs, on the backs of leaflets the VC and NVA scattered around the place.

G.I.—don't shoot. You will return home safely.

Paper as thin as Bible pages. Papa sticking out his bottom lip: *G.I.? Why don't the VC send any letters to us?*

Operation Ranch Hand. Ta much for the field manual, Washington. Patrolling through the defoliated rubber trees. Looked just like the aftermath of a bushfire, before the epicormic growth kicks in. A whole different planet.

True magic. Hand of God, whatever you call it. Felt it sometimes. Like when a mortar fell six feet away and didn't detonate. Why?

. . . all chemical agents used in Vietnam have been fully exonerated from causing veterans' subsequent ill health, with the partial exception of the antimalarial drug Dapsone, whose status has not been resolved . . .

Still have one of those VC leaflets somewhere. On one side it says *U.S. Armymen. Why and for whom are you 10,000 miles from home to live a helluva life and die on this soil?* And on the other there's Reed's fading pencil sketch of a man—a kid, really—cleaning his SLR. Cartoon speech bubble: *Helluva life all right. I'd give my left nut for a Jack 'n' Coke.* Probably would've.

Your Sense of Smell. You will learn rapidly to identify those odors which are common to the battlefield . . . Most chemical agents have very faint odors or none at all.

Hard to describe the stink. Like a fish tank that hasn't been cleaned in a long while. Sometimes in the height of summer there'll be a whiff of an old storm drain, the city's rotten guts, and it comes close to that.

Radioing in for the dustoff, then picking his teeth and jawbone out of the dirt, like he was still going to need them. Crazy thinking. Contagious.

Hiss and stink of piss hitting hot metal, only way to cool the gun barrel.

Souvenirs: Small china duck. Chain of three and a half links. Woman's tortoiseshell comb. Dream of her face at the window. Don't ask.

Finch: *You got twenty dong?*

Papa: *Yeah, but if I wanted it to disappear, I'd go for a stroll in Vung Tau and let a girl get her hand in me pocket.*

They'd medevaced him out in time, but there wasn't much left to work with. That handful of teeth and jawbone—what happened to that? Remember someone saying to put them in an envelope and post it to Johnny Gorton. *Nah, Gorton got his face fucked up when he was RAAF. Send it All the Way to LBJ.*

Blokes losing it over weird shit. Driving over guys in APCs without batting an eyelid, or joking after Finch tripped a Jumping Jack. *For me next trick . . .* But Reed didn't want to say goodbye to his weaselly little pet. Sooking and chucking stones as it rippled off into the jungle.

Coming home to *The Price Is Right* and "I Started a Joke." Coming home to "Ho Ho Ho Chi Minh."

All those months spent charging sandbags, screaming *Nog*, screaming *Gook*. Then Simon says, *Game's over now, son.* Simon says, *Get ya shit and shake hands, boys.*

The first hot shower. Couldn't leave. Even after the water went tepid. Tetch rapping on the door: Knock, knock, knock. Knock, knock, knock. *Mum? I reckon he's died in there.* Could've. It was that good.

Smack was like that. The long, hot bath of it.

Wasn't like he ever bit anyone, just a big kitten, really. But the whiny civvies. So that was that, he had to go. To the zoo, poor fella. *Hell, rather shoot him than send him to the zoo.*

My Lai all over the papers. Calley striding across the front page on his way to Fort Benning. *How can you say you didn't know?* Foxy in the front bar, speaking into his pint. *Well, that's well and truly fucked us. Tarred us all with the same ugly brush.*

Taxi driving, two months. Wouldn't have been so bad except for all the bleeding penitents. Like piloting a confession booth on wheels. *The things I've seen, the things I've done . . .* Boo friggen' hoo.

Word got around that one of the new recruits—drunk as a skunk after a boozer—goes down and *liberates* Kepala. That was the word: *liberate. No zoo for you! No zoo for you!* Don't know if it's a true story, but it's a good story.

Blonde on St. Kilda Beach, high summer. She smelled like a dead thing down there, but did her anyway, it'd been that long. Shaking the sand out of a shoe back at the rooming house and wondering when the clap might set in.

Bricklaying. Three weeks.

Coming to on the floor with a neck ache and half a belt. Should've bought a better brand, an RM Williams. Nothing to do but laugh. And wear a scarf for the next fortnight; never mind it's the middle of a heat wave. Looked like a fag trying to look like John Wayne.

Repat, six weeks. Crossword puzzles. Breadboard for Mum.

TPI, you Nasho muppet? What'd you see we didn't see?

The way people's eyes lit up for Long Tan but stayed dull as dishrags at the mention of Coral-Balmoral. Might as well be talking about a law firm. Stopped talking.

Airless furnace of the projection booth. Trapped up there, and all the time the sound like great wings. Funny, couldn't do it nowadays. Would start sweating at the stairs. But there was something about it then. Bossless. Godlike. Looking down on all those silly buggers cramming Jaffas into the black pits of mouths, laughing popcorn at the big screen.

Saw her running up the steps of the Capitol with her sister. Can't even remember what the film was. *Gone with the Wind? Goodbye, Mr. Chips?* Just looking down through the bio-box porthole for the back of her braided head, nearly missing the cue marks.

Smell of her clean hair. Like something from childhood. Something unreachable. Her pointy, kittenish face before parts of it started to fall.

Passenger seat of the Corvette. Twenty years old and they'd given her that flashy car. A good lot of miles already clocked up on it, but still. Stubble catching on the see-through stuff of her underwear. Said she liked that: manly. Biting through that flimsy mesh to taste her, slick, salty like the sea. She laughed: *Do you know how much these cost?*

The banner that read *Hey Hey LBJ*, and the rest. People marching under it. A woman with a very red, very pretty mouth opened it and said

I am confident the majority of the Australian people will continue to give their support to this policy and will want us to make a measured contribution

Opened it and said two words.

Apple picking in Bathurst. Mangoes in Dimbulah. Oranges in Mildura. Huntsman spiders the size of hubcaps. But Tetch there, the whole season. Shouting pints at the longest bar in the world, sliding them along the sleek dark varnish with his butchered hands. Face cracking readily into a grin. *Glad you came along. Glad you're here.*

Child. Killers.

Her father standing tall on the veranda. Looked like Burt Lancaster, planted there with his feet apart, arms folded. *You go with him, Evvie, and you're cut off.* Watching her walk down the white gravel drive, swinging her big red leather suitcase into the boot of the Corvette.

Cassette tape of Pachelbel's *Canon* and her simple summer dress. Sprig of jasmine pinned into her hair and two brandies at the Young and Jackson. Said that was all she wanted, anyway. Still a game to her, all of it.

Would've thought twice about letting a dog kip in that house. As long as there's a lemon tree, she goes. A lemon tree, and she's apples.

Mind does weird things, trying to distract itself. A bitten tongue or a hummed note. Smoke thrown. Don't look.

A darkness there was no climbing out of. Fists sinking deep into mud walls. But then the dream ended, and it was her body that was so soft.

Tried to leave, get back into repat. Couldn't hurt her from there. Didn't she get it? What the distance was for. But she'd always turn up at the clinic like she was dressed for a party, for high tea. Stockings and everything, red on her lips.

Smoking out front of the hospital when Lani was born. Smoking out front of a different hospital when Ruby was born. All these women in the house. Always wanted a boy, a little mate. Someone to teach how to . . . Don't know. Teach him something. Useful.

Walking out one night after a blue. Ev locking herself in the bedroom. Again. Made it to Pyalong in four hours; then it started pissing down. Lit smokes to keep warm under the bridge, and there she was, the poor mutt, some sight—bits of collie and red kelpie all mongreled up, skinny in her soaked fur and jumping with fleas. Carried her home tucked under the jacket. Probably caught some of her vermin.

Stepping through the door just as everyone was sitting down to Weet-Bix. *Where've you been?* Out tumbles Belle on cue, ta-dah. *Dad, she pongs!* says Ru, but she's squeezing the wretched thing so hard it can hardly get a yip out. Best thing to happen to that little mongrel. That was something. To be someone's best thing.

Q: How many Vietnam veterans does it take to screw in a lightbulb?

"Khe Sanh" on the radio. On the stereo and jukebox. Over the loudspeakers at the supermarket when all a man wants to do is buy a loaf of Tip Top and beat the traffic home before the storm breaks. Even the checkout girl singing along. Asked her, *Know where Khe Sanh is, love?* Nope. At least somebody was making a buck off that mess.

Tacking posters over holes in the walls for the rental inspection. Smarmy realo maggot: *You're not s'posed to hang pictures.* Could've put his head through the wall.

A: How would you know, arsehole? You weren't there.

Like a little kid—couldn't sleep with the blinds closed. Still can't sleep with the blinds closed.

This old digger, in repat. Strange bird they called Clarrie Cryptic, part of the furniture. Decades in that joint, just doing the crosswords from the paper and being flirty to the nurses. Giving them that Laurence Olivier kind of cheek. Dapper, that's what you might call him. Stern part down the left side of his snowy old head. A bit like Ev's old man, without the pole up the arse.

Got recruited, after a fashion. Calling one of the quacks a reprobate.

Know some big words, do you, mate? That was Clarrie. Magpie-eyed, waving his paper over his head.

Can't do them things.

Them *things? Don't act the grunt. You're in here to think differently, aren't you?*

You don't scare me. So sweet, the first time, first real bad night she'd been there for. Almost dumb enough to believe her. But then the words changed their meaning. Sneaky little shits. *You don't scare me.* Meaning: she was scared, all right. White-knuckle scared, hand wrapped round a kitchen knife. *Go on then. Do it. Do it. Fucking Do. It. Woman.*

Seven letters: *Go grabbing Italian smoker in Southeast Asia.*

Tried to quit a hundred times. Whenever they jacked up the price on a pouch of Port Royal. Made it to nearly a fortnight once, all going beaut. Then Ru jumped out from behind a door. *Boo!* Just lost it then.

When Ev got sick. Her beautiful hair falling out. *Alopecia*, like the name for some exotic breed of horse. But it just meant she hid what was left under a yellow babushka scarf and looked twenty years older. Thought it would be better, getting out of the way. Calmer for her, you know.

Rooming house. Fitzroy Street. The place all full of flyspot and damp ghosts. Finch in the corner, grinning with what was left of his jaw. *Hey, Jackrabbit. You got twenty dong?*

Pay phone and Ev singing drunk down the line, *Street boy . . .*

Remember Lani as a tiny kid. Nervous little thing. Pick her up and she'd be trembling, throwing up when someone so much as raised their voice.
   Hey, Ev, what's wrong with this kid? She crook or what?

Alopecian horses. Could just about see them, running golden-syrup circles round the yard. Something her father would've put his money into. The kind of life she should have stayed put in.

Oh, you wonder, do you? You really wonder what's wrong? Bloody mystery, is it?

Repat, only a week or so that time. Fella wandering around a bit frantic, with this little bundle of sticks in a pot of dry dirt, saying not to worry, not to worry, he could save it. He propped it under a busted rain gutter to catch the runoff, and within the week it was showing green. New growth; wasn't he so proud.

Eleven letters: *Eddie's limbo worsened back from war.*

Shrink said to buy a diary, said write it all down. Wrote: *It was hot, and we were sick of survival biscuits. NCOs assured us that the biscuits would survive, even if we didn't. The photographs we kept on us fell to bits cause of all the rain and all the sweat.* Then tore out the first page and gave the diary to Ru for scribbling in.

Future. Couldn't get a handle on it. Nights when the future was only what the headlights could pick up, and no farther.

You. Are. Going. To. Make. It. Up. To. These. Girls. You. Are. Going. To. Make. It. Up. To. Us. Believe you me.

Just wanted to take her somewhere. Nice. Away from it all. Got it almost good. Almost perfect. The caravan, the Yarra Yarra, where it's still crystal, before it starts flowing arse up. Not a soul around. The girls on their own holiday at Stell's. Waking up Ev with tea and Scottish oats cooked on the Sterno. Lying in late, remembering each other. Almost something good enough to point back to and say *Now wasn't that something.* Fat, lazy river slapping at its banks and riddled with glinting trout.

Just that last part, with the car running out of petrol, things sliding off the rails. Fighting in the sick light of the Mobil, knocking over a chips display, people staring. *Sir, you'll have to—* yeah fucken' yeah. But almost, almost.

Ru wanting help with her grade-three geography project. A hundred fucked-out, sucked-out countries they could've given her. Why that one? *Drew it from a hat,* she says. *What's the weather like? Staple foods? How do you say hello?*

How should I know?

They'd teach a four-year-old to pull the pin. Wire him up, then say, Now you go over there and say hello to those big funny-looking men. And so you just wouldn't . . .

Let me repeat, in simple terms

A kid would totter right out onto the range and you just wouldn't . . .

Let me repeat, in simple terms

Seven letters. *Incontinent men suffering memory loss.*

You just wouldn't know.

Remember standing in the doorway, watching the girls sleep. *Please be okay. Please be okay.*

A roll of half-shot 35mm coiled up like a viper in the camera. Eleven years in the bottom of the duffel, coiled up like that. Couldn't trust it. Couldn't even remember what was on it. Might've been temples and rubber trees. Pictures in the clouds, guys slouching under slouch hats, just lying around, bored, brainless. Village kids, drowsy buffalo. Skinny girls in dark rooms and silk underwear. Remember the weight of the Minolta, the leather strap getting sticky in the humidity. And Reed helping to thread the film onto the tiny white toothy wheels. Just not what was shot on it.

Found it lying there on the kitchen table. Careful lettering, graylead lines showing through red and yellow headings. *Population. Staple Foods.* Drawings of a bowl of rice, noodles, a skeleton fish. The words for *hello.* The words for *goodbye. From 1955 to 1975 there was a war there and my dad was in it. The mosquitoes were awful, and he missed home.* Took it out into the backyard before she woke up for school.

Oh, that was low, you bully. Even for you that was low . . .

Welcome home, temazepam! Welcome home, Valium! Welcome home, clozapine! That's a parade. Wave your own bloody flag.

67

*. . . a consequence of alcohol and tobacco consumption and of the
stresses of the Vietnam War (some of them peculiar to that war) . . .*

Sweating all the way to the chemist, guts twisted up. But the old
guy just shakes his head and hands over an envelope of blanks.
Twenty-four frames of nothingness. *Guess it wasn't wound on
properly.* Walked back out into the shopping center car park, and
there it all was, sudden. True magic, all right. Like a slide reel
behind the eyes. Foxy drinking from a boot after losing a bet.
Reed's mongoose going to town on a hunk of cheese. The B-52
crater, water at the bottom stained to red muck. Counted
forty-two. Then the bulldozers came and covered it all over.

Repat, four weeks. Leatherwork. Birdhouse.

Trying to say sorry with objects. Evelyn: stockings. Tetch: cigarettes (tailors 'cause he makes an embarrassment of rollies).
Lani: fuck knows. Ru: those weird horror books she likes. *Too
old for them now,* Ev says later. *Good try, though.*

Hitting a wombat just outside Blackwood, driving the girls up to
visit Mum.

*Dad? Dad! We've gotta go back. Even if it's dead, we've gotta
check the pouch.*

Wombats don't have pouches, Possum Chops.

They do. Turn around. We've gotta go back and check.

Can't stop. They got claws like razors. A sick one'll rip you to bits.

Go on, then. Fucken' look, then: skinny arms still reaching out
to someone. Black cotton pajamas ripped open at the stomach.
You gonna check what he had in that basket?

Can we not and say we did?

Jesus, I'll do it. Reed holding up—what was it that time? A
chook. A frag. A tin of rice. Don't remember.

When you think of happiness, what picture do you have in your mind?

   You already asked that one.

   But you declined to answer.

Ev backed up against the door. Lani nine years old and getting in between. Already, that look in her eyes, her hands making sharp little fists. *Hate you, hate you.* Thought: Yeah me too, love; me too.

Brighton Beach like a carnival. Fried sugar and vinegar smells floating from food vans down to the shore, thickening the salt air. Little kids belting around barefoot, spraying up the powdery sand, belonging to no one, it seems. Huddle of Scots or fake Scots, all arms-thrown-round-shoulders and "Auld Lang Syne," but it's just past ten—still a couple of hours to go yet. Past this.

Pay phone outside the yacht club. Could call her. Say *Happy New Year, baby.* Then what?

Waiting for the city to explode. Counting down, so it can't creep up. Gatling guns and red mines. Like the rain drumming the car roof, all those things that are lost forever, all those things that can't ever be good again. Watching the sky turn dusty yellow, trapping the light and spreading it out above the beach like an old blanket. Smothering.

Out here years ago, when both the girls were tiny. A day where nobody could've told just by looking. Where anybody would've looked and thought: Family. Sandwiches still cool in their foil, red fizz and icy beer. Hot chips, Ev licking salty oil from her fingers. Wading out past the breakers with Ruby and Lani, one hanging off each arm. Showing them how to somersault, out there where the water was over their heads. *Gimme your foot, then*, and them clambering up to be launched skyward, *hup-hup-hup!*

Ev walking out along the breakwall, pale cotton skirt wisping round her legs, shading the sun from her eyes with a forearm. *Mum! Come in.* But she's smiling and shaking her head because no, she's turning gold. Turning twenty. As if there has never been one bad year. That close. That life other people are living, right there within shouting distance. Then cupping her hands around her mouth and calling out across the water, *All right, you three . . .*

Calls us in. Us. Calls us home.

IV
Flight Mode

FAKE SNOW CAUGHT HER HAIR, LIKE FESTIVE DANDRUFF. LANI ruffles it out. *Tender Prey* on the portable stereo, skipping on a scratch. Half out of her clothes, these red licks all down her legs from doubling up on Will's Honda in a skirt too short to shield her from the whipping scrub. Now it looks like she's been belted a few rounds with the iron cord. But that was years ago, the iron cord. Lately it's fists if it's anything, if her mother can gather the energy, though most of the fight has gone out of her these past few weeks. Something's up; now she's sleeping later, flipping out less. No more screaming through Lani's locked bedroom door. No more being dragged out of bed by a handful of her hair at four a.m. because the dishes haven't been done or the rubbish hasn't been wheeled to the roadside. If Evelyn's got a problem, she takes it to the rabbits, out of earshot. Muttering like a madwoman while the pink-eyed bunnies blink back at her from their pokey hutch. Lani could just about hug them.

She wets a finger in her mouth and traces one of the angry welts across her shin. Wonders if every moment she moves through will mark her somehow. This time, at least, she's glad to have proof. It felt good, safe, pressed up against him, fingertips laddering his ribs through his T-shirt. The night rushing at them so fast her eyes teared up. She'd wanted him to keep riding, all night, right up to the border. Sleep by the river. Any river. Anyplace that wasn't home. But he'd turned off the highway and onto her road, past the few neighboring houses with their spooky, lonely television glow seeping through closed blinds. Will pulled over just short of the house, and she climbed off, didn't argue. He must have sensed her disappointment, though, and misread it.

I'd take you closer, you know, but your dad. He'd probably lob a grenade at me.

I told you, she said, unthreading the helmet strap from where it bit into her chin. He's gone.

Yeah, but he's gotta come back sometime.

She'd shrugged and handed him back his helmet. Anyway, he's not the one to worry about, believe me. Thanks for the ride. And she walked toward the house, holding her breath in the flood of quiet that came before the kick of the engine.

He'd reappeared toward the end of November, just materialized in place of his father in the mechanics shed. She'd missed the bus and was scuffing the forty minutes home in her clompy Oxfords, and there he was, re-chroming parts of Mack Ferguson's pristine Velocette that not one soul had ever seen the man ride.

Lani remembered Will at fourteen; he'd had a sort of helpless, unfinished look back then, downy buzz cut and wet marsupial eyes. When his folks split, his mother whisked him off to live in Auckland. Lani had imagined spearfishing (true) and snowboarding (also true) and had flared up with envy for an instant and just as quickly forgotten about it. About him. Now, in his dad's workshop, he was kneeling over a bucket, wearing a face mask and thick rubber gloves, like for dishes or strangulation. Hair brushing the collar of a T-shirt that might have been black once, now grayed with wear, a Rorschach of sweat showing between his shoulder blades. Will turned around then, had maybe felt her gawking, and she saw the glint of a barbell through his brow. That wouldn't fly here, wouldn't last long. She was two years younger, and she could've told him that much. It seemed a stupid thing to say, though, a bad way to start. She couldn't think up anything better, but he saved her from having to. Raised his gloved hand and squinted under it, then swiped his dust mask away against his shoulder.

Hey, he said. Lana Burroughs.

Lani.

Right. You shot up. He left the headlight casing submerged in its chemical bath and stepped into the daylight, unpeeling his gloves.

He gave her a look she couldn't read, then came out with it: Is it true what people've been saying?

She felt a little stab in her stomach about what he might have meant. Was it true she'd had an abortion? No, just glandular fever. That her uncle was an ex-con? That was only talk, though sometimes she wished it were true. Then Tetch would be weird interesting instead of just weird weird. Was Matt D. true, was Jarrod Blackwood true, was Marshall Weste true? Yes, yes, and almost. Not quite, with Weste; he hadn't been able to finish, so they'd sat there quiet for a while, passing a smoke back and forth between them until Weste punched the bricks like an idiot and skinned his knuckles. Later he'd tried to get his whole hand in, as if to settle things that way. But whose business was any of it?

What? she asked. She untucked her school shirt, hot now and near bored.

What happened with your dog and all that.

For a moment she felt relieved, and then ashamed for feeling relieved. Yeah, she told him, it was revolting.

Sorry, he said. Think I kinda remember that dog. Dad says he's heard of lambs ripped up pretty bad.

She couldn't tell if he was taking the piss. Where were there sheep around here? He'd been gone four years. She looked for the fourteen-year-old in him—the scrawny BMX rat with the rusty crust around his nostrils from constant nosebleeds. But that kid was gone, or pretty well disguised under work-stained Levis and the faded tour shirt of some Kiwi punk band. He wasn't joking, she decided, just confused maybe.

Reckon the government will get onto it one day, he was saying. Wait and see—sooner or later some ag minister will be throwing their weight at it, tuning in to all the crackpots like it was the last thylacine.

She blew air through her teeth and let that go for an answer. Nobody spoke much of politicians in her house, of what they might do. Only what might be done to them: grisly stuff.

So you're just back for a visit, she guessed, and Will shrugged, glancing back at the dismantled bike.

School's done. Dad's sick. Made sense. Then he told her he'd meant to travel after finishing school, backpack South America. But there wasn't the cash for it, anyway, and his old man had to get to dialysis twice a week.

But Argentina, Colombia. Not like they're going to dry up and blow away, hey? He was looking at her legs: long, bruised, brown enough. Her school socks had slid halfway down her shins on the walk, exposing the still-pink flick of a scar where an ignition key had crushed into her knee over winter. Swinging the wheel on Matt's old man's ruined Datsun, her eyes closed, driving just to crash.

The uniforms they make you gooses wear . . . Where I went, we just wore whatever. Anything we liked. You could dye your hair blue if you wanted and nobody would give you a second look.

She didn't point out that he'd once had to suffer the same uniform. But she did tell him then, about the barbell.

He'd only grinned at her. We'll see, hey?

She doesn't want to risk the bathroom, a collision with Evelyn in the hallway—she'll just get roped into doing some other thing— so settles for dry-shaving her legs in the privacy of her room. One of her father's disposable plastic razors, a cheapo that'll take skin with it here and there if she's not careful. She rinses her shins with squirts from a water bottle, brushes the last of the fake snow from her hair. Tonight there'll be a bonfire, a lot of booze, a dozen ways of leaving without leaving. Trina with some sweet-awful rocket fuel to rinse out the bitter grit.

The dress is a knee-length Lurex halter, split to show thigh. Wet-looking, backless. No bra, then. Not like there's much to hold up anyway. She'd seen Trina wearing it once, the dress, and what it did to her. Who it made her into. It had taken a flask of snaffled bourbon and an English essay to wrangle it for tonight.

Worth it, Lani figures, watching herself in the narrow mirror on the back of the door, writhing a bit, like dancing without trying too hard. Glitter gumming her eyelashes together, purple mascara streaking her hair. There was an idea of what she was supposed to look like. This isn't it, really, but it's as close as she's getting. (Aunt Stell at Christmas, saying, You look so much like your mum at your age, but so much . . . I don't know. Older? You always look so tired, honey.

Yeah, well. My mother didn't have my mother as a mother. She'd said something like that.)

She packs a bag with a pair of skinny pink heels, makeup patiently filched from the chemist, lipstick so dark it's nearly black. A green plastic pillbox filled with her father's meds, all of them jumbled in together. Sampler.

Rolled into a pair of socks rolled into a drawer, the bundle of autumn-colored bank notes. Always in dreams she's kicking up money among crinkling leaves and chip packets rustling in the gutters. Of course it never happens that way. Some of the bundle is from pushing the meds, but most of it comes from the grandfolks, care of Stell. Ghostfolks, Lani calls them; she wouldn't know them if she met them in the street. *On the hush, now . . .* Enough there for a bus ticket to Sydney and a week of floating up there, if she wants, though that's not what they'd meant it for. Or maybe they had, who really knew.

Outside, the squeal and shudder of the garage roller door going up. Evelyn hauling Christmas junk out there. *Conclusively,* she'd repeated this morning. Tests to prove *conclusively.* That Lani was not her father's child. But Lani had been overhearing this story since before she'd known what *conclusively* even meant, and the shock of it, the hurt of it had more or less been worn away. Anyway, it turned out she was. Anyway, what it really means, this story her mother tells over and over, is *Be on my side. Get in my corner.*

But she's never been able to stand corners. She spins the volume up on "Sugar Sugar Sugar" and escapes through the slit window mesh.

She reaches the Ark early, dropping into the narrow slice of shade it throws. *Ark* is only a name people give it; really it's the ferro-cement hull of a ship, propped up in the middle of someone's fallow paddock, way back from the road. It makes no sense out here, hours and hours from any water deep enough for it to belong in. And at the same time it makes a kind of sense, follows a kind of dream logic, having been here longer than herself or any of her family, its iron struts bubbled with vibrant rust, sunk down into the baked earth. Whether it's an abandoned project or somebody's idea of a joke, it's everyone's now. The town's unofficial guest book, all graffed over with tags and postcodes and who was here in '74, '78, '83, etc., and who sux cox and what their phone numbers are or used to be. And above it all, in big orange house-paint letters: *The End Shall Come With A Flood.* Sometimes there are cows nosing about under the Ark, bubblegum tongues stretching out for the wedge of grass that stays green in its shadow. It does look biblical then.

Lani swaps her boots for heels and stashes her bag in the shade, she and the Ark both looking out of place, waiting together for something to happen. Something to lift them up and carry them elsewhere. Just this feeling, this inkling. Like maybe there are places in the world that don't intend to press you flat, grind you out between the sky and the earth. The world is getting smaller; even she can see that much, even from out here. Or the spaces between people are getting smaller, the distances. Shrinking.

She listens for Will's Honda, but there's no engine noise at all. Just the rushing sound of the grass and its cicadas, all of it oceanlike. She keeps time, making a maraca of her father's pills in their green plastic box. She can't remember the proper names for all of them—the two-colored capsule ones and the round vanilla-yellow ones with the cross etched into the top. The tiny blue pills with hard, glossy shells like baby M&M's, but the insides dusty white and bitter. These her mother crushes up with spoonfuls of honey when Ru can't sleep.

Mum, you can't give that stuff to kids.

Excuse me, madam, you're the expert now, are you?

Ru standing in the doorway, swamped in an oversize T-shirt nightie, hair a rat's nest. Glaring, like *Who asked you?*

Fine.

The pills, tranqs, all do different versions of the same thing: tranquilize. As though their dad's a dangerous animal escaped from somewhere. When he takes them, half his lights go out— *bang!*—and he just wants to sit in his chair and watch reruns of old Paul Newman movies.

They muck up me thinking, he complains of the pills. But every single time Mum asks him what he's thinking about, meds or no meds, he just blinks at her like a buffalo and says, Nothin'.

In the years before Ru—or the years before Ru can probably remember—there were sometimes coin tricks. A copper one-cent piece rubbed and rubbed against Dad's elbow while he told a story about the shy possum, and when the story was over, both possum and coin had disappeared. *Kerpoof.* She remembers, too, animal faces drawn in blue biro on the shells of hard-boiled eggs—the childish curling *W*s of cat mouths and the sharp *V*s of bird beaks—so that when she opened the fridge to sneak a mouthful of condensed milk cold from the can, there'd be a miniature zoo lined up inside the door, staring back at her accusingly. A little egg-animal jury.

In those days he'd found kinder ways of getting away. Fossicking trips to the salvage yard with Uncle Tetch for electrical bits and pieces, or mushroom hunting through the pine plantation and along the nearby windbreaks. A couple of times he'd thought to take Lani instead, the two of them rugged up against the autumn chill, sifting under the dripping trees for the alien forms that nudged up overnight from the damp carpet of needles. *Slippery Jacks.* She thought he was fibbing about the name, whose suspect caps were sickening to look at and worse to touch, sometimes with millipedes or other crawlies caught in their goo. Who would eat those?

I would, her dad told her, taking a raw chomp out of one to make her squeal. But it was the pine mushies they were mostly after anyway, a poisonous-looking orange, and if you weren't careful and broke the gills, they stained your hands like monster blood.

He didn't mind. He was different out there. Easier. Funny, even, telling her his nonsense jokes.

All right, missy, you tell me: What would you rather be or a policeman? A question that called for no sensible answer.

At first it stumped her, but then she caught on: I'd rather be a Polly Waffle. An octopus's walking stick.

But then he'd go all serious. Don't you ever go picking these without me, you hear? You get mixed up, pick the wrong kind, you'll go to sleep and never wake up again.

She'd shake her head for no as he carefully swept back the needles and twisted the thing up by the stalk, placing the prize in her spread hands so that she could deliver it to the newspaper-lined basket. Brushing her fingertips along the gills on the way: monster blood.

At home he cooked them up with salt and browned butter, stinking the house out till it smelled rich and earthy as a burrow. And though they may as well have been slugs for how slimy they were—and how they tasted, for that matter—she'd pretended they were just as good as marshmallows and eaten them anyway, as many bites as she could stand, because she wanted him to know that she liked the things he liked. Because she wanted to prove, *conclusively*, and because she didn't want to be left behind the next time he went out to the pines swinging that basket.

But not long after she started school, his gatherings turned into wanderings, and his wanderings turned into *fucked-off-agains*—and these *fucked-offs* might be measured in days or in weeks. Then later, in months, spanning birthdays and holidays. And it wasn't always easy to tell which would be which when he went out the door. Because at first, when he was starting to go bad, all he ever took was his wallet. Though sometimes her mother would raise her eyebrows as the flyscreen banged closed behind him, and she'd mouth the word *Go*, so Lani would, right after him, one night bolting out in her summer pajamas and purple rabbit slippers. Earlier there'd been a fight, and a few broken things made of glass, so she wasn't allowed to walk in the kitchen, and she didn't properly remember the rest of what had happened in there. After a while, all those squalls had rolled into one another. But she remembers scarpering outside that particular evening. How it had just finished raining, the world misty-quiet and gray with the last of the light, the insects on pause and the dirt road trickling with little errant streams. She pelted along it, and when she caught her father, he pulled up sharp, whirled around on her.

Go home, he said, pointing back to where home was or should be.

She could feel the wetness of the road soaking up through her slippers. Heard her voice shake when she answered him, I'll go home if you go home.

Not going to happen, Kiddo. He turned and kept walking, and she shadowed him.

Jesus, he said. Your mother put you up to this, didn't she? You should be in bed.

She had been put up to it, but she said nothing. Just ghosted alongside him, a smatter of steps for each of his long strides, the night coming down quiet around them and the road rising gently to meet the highway. Clouds raced across the face of the moon, veiling and unveiling it, though no breeze found them down there on earth.

How far is it?

How far is what?

Where we're going? She asked only to say something; she knew where he was headed—or had been, before she caught him. The station, which stood a little way out of town, where trains rarely found reason to stop. He would wait there, two hours, six hours, however long. Or maybe he'd hitch to Melbourne with one of the trucks or someone driving back from a holiday up north.

But tonight he said, Oh, bloody hell. A man can't even take a frigging walk. And this time, at least, he turned for home. The road had drunk up the rain and was mucky in places. He looked down at her feet, and so did she, at the bedraggled ears of her slippers. No chance of those coming back into the house.

I suppose you'll want to be carried now.

She did want that—her feet were pinging with the icy needles that arrive shortly before numbness. But it seemed important to say no, and so she said no, and he didn't fight her on it, accepting her refusal with a nod and a cough.

Her father was slower, walking back. No timetable in his head, no train to make or to miss. Lani kept pace with him easily, slopping along in her ruined slippers, triumphant. From somewhere came the gurgle of frog talk. She wanted to say something too, but couldn't think what. Something encouraging. When nothing came to her, she took hold of his jacket sleeve to let him know that there were no hard feelings.

There would be many nights afterward where she could not turn him around, where there was nothing she could say or do to shame the rage out of him, bring him home. The last time she even tried—though she was thirteen then and had more or less given up on him by that stage—she shadowed him toward the highway, silent except for when she asked him for a cigarette and he rolled one for her in the pitch dark. They bobbed along, closer in gait now, her legs nearly as long as his, and in place of talk there was the hiss and flare of tobacco, the twin glowing ends that seemed conversation enough, until she felt the road sloping up beneath her feet and she told him, It's me who cops it, you know? When you're not around.

Even in the dark he wouldn't look at her. She could tell that, hear it. His head still turned to the highway, his voice aimed down at the road when he said, I know, love. I'm sorry. But there isn't much I can do about it, hey.

•

She let him walk on alone to the station that would sometimes dream up a train for him to leave on.

She squints toward the stand of pines. Those mushrooms don't grow there anymore. Either kind. She's looked. Maybe the weather is wrong for them. Or maybe they do grow there and something else always gets to them first. That'd be right.

Will—of course he's found something better to do, somebody more interesting to do it with. Those stories he has of trekking all over the South Island. Hitching most of the ride with a couple of Maori punk girls in an old converted ambulance, getting nipped at by their contraband pet stoat, Baby Marmite. Breakfasts of stolen servo pastries—microwaved, they were that cocky. Night swimming stoned under cold stars and falling asleep to the thrash of the ocean. He still wears a jagged seal tooth around his neck, scooped up from the black sand at Piha. Crabeater, *crenulated*, like a lick of flame carved from bone, threaded onto leather. That same beach had later snapped him from the strap of a board and flung him into the rocks. Two weeks in a coma, he'd told her, and now the only thing that could scare him was the thought of ever being forced to lie that still again.

Can't be much better being here, she'd answered, petulant. Knowing it wasn't his choice to be: he'll leave when he can, and even if he stays long enough, he'll get bored of her. The farthest she's ever been in her life is Lakes Entrance, which Ru—only little then—summed up as looking better in fridge magnets.

The other options for tonight are too bleak to ponder. Watching *Rage* with Mum, playing Monopoly with Ru. If she'd planned ahead, she could've snuck a lift to the city, bringing down seven shades of strife at home, but it's too late for that anyway, she's stuck here now.

She mouths the words of a poem Mim had tricked her into learning by heart. (Five minutes, Lah. How long is five minutes? Just as long as it takes Maud to get into the garden, love; on you go.) A distraction Lani later used with Ru when the folks were in demolition mode. She'll give Will until *larkspur*. She meanders through it four times before she hears the thrum of the Honda, and a moment later Will crests the rise.

He props the bike and falls into the shade beside her, still fumbling with his helmet. Sorry, he says. Got called in on Dad duty. When he pulls the helmet off, she sees that the barbell has been knocked from his brow, the skin there split like soft fruit.

She shakes the box of pills at him for hello. Lose a fight?

Just a footy match. He grins. You get the names of those?

He'll care?

Will shrugs. Aiden, I reckon he'll care. Everyone else—most people—will just take whatever they're given.

Okay, well. This one's Valium, definitely, and this is temazepam—pretty much the same, isn't it? And I don't know what these little shits are. She spills a few out into her palm, and he shrugs again.

But they're all benzos, right?

I guess, yeah.

Not exactly social stuff, but like I said, people out here will just swallow—that's if we're even headed to the same party. Those the only shoes you got?

Telling him to go chase himself would be the right answer, she knows, but her mouth feels too dry even to laugh.

Well, he says, uneasy now. So long as she doesn't conk out halfway, yeah? Oh, hey. I brought something.

From the bike's dusty pannier he takes out a little rocket-looking thing, red and silver. Soda thingummy, for whipped cream. She knows that much.

Used to be my nan's, he says, digging around in the pannier for a cardboard box of what look like miniature torpedoes. Let me get you set up, and he loads one into the soda thing and twists until there's a muffled crack and hiss—whatever it is escaping from the tiny bomb. Condensation clouding then beading up the metal.

Laughing gas, like dentists use, Will explains. Like sucking the helium out of a balloon, yeah? But you just take it straight from the siphon. You'll want to be sitting down, probably.

Lani breathes as she's told, cold fog blooming in her lungs. Then tipping back just as the sky pulls away. Like plunging into a deep pool somewhere down inside her own body. Toward the surface of herself, she's aware of him above her, going *skksh tsh tsh* in her ear. Underwater noises, the whistle and tick of crays, yabbies, rivermud creatures. Peaceful. She could stay down at the silty bottom. Doesn't want to leave, to come back. But back she comes anyway. Floating up from that great depth and breaking surface in the paddock of summer grass where he's stopped making the noises and her mouth has run drier still. When she opens her eyes, she sees him watching her, the way a person might watch an animal dream, as if she's a cat with twitching paws.

Why'd you do that? she asks him.

Huh?

Like crickets or something. She tries to make the noise, *sk sksh sksh.*

I don't know. Someone did it for me once. It just makes it . . .
I don't know. Nicer.

Can I go again?

Doesn't last long enough, does it? Here, I'll come with you.
He feeds the siphon two of the bombs. Again the hush of air into
the chamber, and he lets her take the first lungful. She hands the
siphon up to him, and a moment later he's there beside her; she's
sure she feels the dirt ripple when he falls back against it.

Back down in it, at the bottom of things, she remembers
something. No, it's not remembering. More like going there. To
something that has already happened and is still happening.
Years ago. But now as well. People talking about her in the next
room, wherever that room might be. And what they're saying, it's
nothing, really—*what eventuates is the capacity, the tendency for
remanence decay; you copy it ten, a dozen times*—just auditory
junk she's picked up, kept stashed up there for some unfathom-
able reason. Like a radio scanned in from somewhere, but she
knows each word the instant before it's said. Something she's
already dreamed, maybe. She feels the weight of Will's hand on
her stomach, the twitch of her leg, the hauling up. And she fights
it, needs to hear the rest, even if she can't make sense of it. Stirring the murky bottom, thrashing about down there for something she can wrap a hand around, but there's nothing, nothing
solid enough to grasp, and she can't bring any of it to the surface,
good or bad. By the time she comes back to the paddock, the sky,
the Ark looming up over them, all the details have smudged
away. There's just the leftover feel of it. A strange, sinister taste
in her mouth.

Again? Will asks.

She shakes her head. I'm done, she says, venturing a leg out
of the Ark's shadow to test the sun's bite.

We'll make a move, then. In a minute. Just let me get my head straight. And they're quiet for a while in the lengthening shade.

The house stands well out from town, halfway to the next, and though she's never been taken there before, she knows it. Everyone does. Things go on out there. All sorts. Past what was once the reservoir, now just a stagnant pool with floating beer cans, rubbish, and the land around it a dumping ground for wrecked or stolen cars, all their ID numbers scratched away.

The way there is rutted by stubborn tree roots and by tires that churned it up in bad weather. Will threads the Honda around the worst of it, the road tossing the bike around, Lani's arse lifting from the pillion as they take the smaller potholes, dust powdering her shins. Shattered wing mirrors wink out at her, flashing gold in the last of the sun, as though signaling for someone.

Long before they get in sight of the place, the party reaches out to meet them, the pulse of bass in the dirt, oily bonfire smoke in spite of the fire ban.

That'll bring pigs.

Cops?

Nah, actual pigs. He laughs. Yeah, cops.

The fire, it eats everything. As Lani and Will pull up, people are feeding it beer cartons and chairs and a pair of skate shoes someone was stupid or stoned enough to have taken off. They're melting at the bonfire's heart, like an offering. Sparks dancing up above the roof of the house.

It's only just dark. Black plumes of flying foxes spilling overhead like fast ink, but their screeching is lost to the sound system—a lot of industrial yellow electrical cables snaking up through a window into the house. Aiden's house, but he's nowhere.

Fireside, people's faces glow like Halloween masks, orange, blue-black in the shadows. Lani searches for Trina among the grim versions of girls she knows but not well enough to talk to, or knows better than to talk to. A little coven of them standing back from the eyelash-curling heat. These girls with hair so sleek it moves like liquid, slips from ties. Eyeing her coolly, *We know what you aren't*, before folding back in on themselves.

The borrowed dress clings to her ribs, and underneath there's her heart thudding like a bird trapped in a box, the way she and Ru had caught a sparrow once, pouncing on it in the garage. Placing their four hands on the shoebox to keep the bird from escaping. The feel of it crashing around beneath, hurting itself. Until quiet. And when they finally lifted the box, it was gape-beaked and still, stunned, creamy chest puffing with small, quick terror.

Will's hand is pressed between her shoulder blades, his flask pressed into her hand. She swallows—rum—and lets him lead her away from the fire, from the crush of people, music she doesn't know and doesn't care to, spikes of her shoes stabbing into the dirt. Stupid. She takes a deeper swallow from the flask.

They find him far back from the house, past the rusting husks of old cars and the single strand of wire poked through palings to mean *fence*. Aiden. Way back where the party is diffused to a dull throb under the grass, light through the trees. Holding on to a rabbit rifle, his long, dark hair as silky as a girl's, but he'd once pulled someone's face down into his knee for saying something like that, and they'd come up with their nose mashed. He's careless with the rifle, swinging it as he would a stick. Picking fruit bats out of the sky like he's pointing out constellations: Orion, the Big Dog, the False Cross . . .

Will says his name.

Hang on a tick.

The crack of the rifle rings out, and a black rag drops from the sky, from its flock. The rag flaps around in the long grass, crying, and then is still.

Nobody says anything. Then Will does: You gonna make sure it's dead, or what?

Nup, hate them things. And when Aiden turns, he sees Lani there.

Sorry, he says. Where's my manners? Holding the rifle out to her. Wanna shot?

She shakes her head. I'll be right, thanks.

You never shot? It's easy but. Go on, I'll show you how.

I'm right, she says again. Just wanted to . . .

All business, hey? He gives her an oily wink, untucking a twenty from his shirt pocket, and Lani swaps it for a handful of the pills that are meant to keep her father calm.

They're—

Not asking what they are, Aiden says.

Careful, Will says. Don't wanna spend your New Year's curled up in bed . . .

Bit of it, why not? And his laugh is terrible. She hopes they do flake him out, the pills.

Aiden looks at Lani then, dead-on, as though he's heard her thoughts. This shit's not my kind of fun, though. Oh, hey, sorry about your mongrel bitch. Leaving just enough space there be-tween *mongrel* and *bitch*. She blinks at him, holds his eye half a heartbeat before her own gaze wavers, then drops. His boots look flayed, laces gone, tongues lolling.

Nah, truly, he says. His voice gone drowsily gentle, almost pillow talk. Accept my condolences and all that.

•

He's not really such an arsehole, Will says, walking her back up to the house. Or didn't use to be. Shit happens, you know.

Behind them the rifle shots resume. She asks what kind of shit, and Will elaborates—by *shit* he means skidding out one night on a loosely graveled back road outside Wallan, Aiden's leg folding under the bike and the exhaust pipe melting right through the skin of his thigh. He means hours unconscious on the bitumen, and blood poisoning, followed by ever-increasing strengths of painkillers, a steady trading up of opioids—pethidine to morphine to heroin—long after the leg had healed around all its pins, skin left like cling wrap where the pipe fell and lay pressed against it all that time.

They climb back over the single-strand fence. A couple of boys are grappling shirtless in a dry plastic kiddie pool while their friend stands by shouting through cupped hands, Any takers? Any takers?

How are you traveling? Will asks her.

Okay.

A couple of hours, and if you're not having fun, we can pike. Couple hours. Okay.

The year starts easily enough, with the spatter of homemade fireworks, all the amateur pyros lighting up what they've concocted out of lawn mower diesel and fertilizer or whatever, stuff pilfered from their fathers' sheds. Dogs going berserk for miles, yapping their heads off. Something will ignite, she knows. And it does, but when it does, it's nothing drastic, only a bottlebrush tree that someone is quick and sober enough to douse with a butchered garden hose.

Lani watches as the bonfire grows to become as big as a room—you could just about live in it—and on the other side, Aiden is licking up one of her dad's pills from an open palm, cat-like, then tonguing it into the mouth of the girl beside him. Nerida. Slacked back in a camping chair, all spangly pink tank top and denim cutoffs, looking dreamy. Too many, already. Who is that dumb? Trina had once convinced her to eat warm wax, swearing that it would line her stomach better than cream, and the little fool had gone for it. Afterward they'd watched her throwing up Veet-laced bourbon into a patch of hydrangeas, telling themselves they had done her a favor of sorts, that she would probably think again in future . . . But apparently no, she would not.

Aiden catches Lani's eye across the fire. Flashes her a conspiratory sort of smile, like she's in on something, and she looks away.

She's good at booze. Usually she is. Since year eight, smuggling vodka into class in a Fanta bottle or a ginger ale bottle, bourbon into cola, whatever she could lay her hand to. Sneaking doses through maths—especially maths—just enough to quiet down the panic and let her drift through, failing calculus in a syrupy haze. Inking brumbies and turbulent rivers of song lyrics across the graph paper, so if Mr. K. looks up, she'll look busy.

But tonight she keeps losing herself midsentence. Coming to among strangers, in conversations she can't remember the beginning of. People watching her, impatient, waiting for her to hurry up and spit it out. Each time she feels that trapped bird, feels the bat plummeting from the blue-black sky, from its liquid flock. How it fell. How fast. She feels that falling over and over.

Somewhere, she knows that each of these conversations is only starting, or hasn't even begun yet—a secret about time that she'd pulled down with the nitrous gas. She thinks she might be able to get back and eavesdrop on herself so that she'd know what to answer now.

You can tell, hey, this kid is saying, too close to her face. A stringy, myxomatosis-looking fucker.

What?

Like, the way the skin is peeled back? Away from the bone? A feral cat won't do that. A fox won't do that.

She doesn't want to agree with him. Not on anything at all. It wasn't like that, she tells him, looking over her shoulder, wondering where Will has disappeared to. Across the fire, Aiden is helping that girl Nerida up the back steps. No, not helping. Dragging. She's kind of melted on him, being half danced, half hauled in a wharfie's waltz that takes her through the screen door. Is that right? Doesn't seem right, but no one's paying them any mind.

I took a photo once, thought I got it, says the rabbity kid. Dead sure that I had it, but it must've moved quicker than the shutter could. Wanna know what I reckon?

He's blinking fast with pink-rimmed eyes. Like he's a camera himself, snapping everything up. She steps away from him, and the backyard tilts. Like that ride at Luna Park—what's the name of it, what's the name of it?—when the floor falls away and you're stuck there to the wall. That's how it is.

Whoa. The rabbity kid reaches his arm out to steady her, but she shakes him off. Her legs are quaky foal legs, but she walks on them anyway, stumbling between the clusters of drinkers on her way toward the house.

The bath is a dozen bags of servo ice turned liquid: wet cardboard and floating labels, bottles of beer and cider soaked brandless. Lani fishes a bottle out of the soup, bangs the cap off on the edge of the sink. Swallows slow, tasting nothing. Steam-warped porn mags stacked inside a yellow milk crate next to the tub, stuck open at their centerfolds. Girls with tattoos of butterflies and tiger lilies flanking their shaved pussies. She flips through them. Everything lying right out like that, for anyone to rummage through. She opens the medicine cabinet on generations of pharmaceutical junk. Rusted tins of pomade and Vaseline, oily-labeled bottles that might've been sitting there half a century. Waterbury's Compound. Magic Silver White. Expired condoms and sticky-looking razor blades dusted with rust and grayish powder. A tray of sewing needles with darkened, sterilized tips. Squashed pill packets with prescriptions for a dozen different names. Lani squints to read the pharmacy labels, looking for Aiden, circa bike accident. Not methadone, but the softer stuff. Pethidine and whatever else. She navigates by the fluoro warning stickers—*Do not drive a vehicle, Do not operate heavy machinery*—shaking out a small deck of blister packs. What she wants is a box, innocent-looking—aspirin or ibuprofen. Something no one would think suss if they saw her walking out with it. Or a soft pack of tissues, that'd work, but there's nothing. She tears strips from the magazines, folds the pills inside makeshift envelopes. These she tucks down into the toes of her shoes, leaning against the edge of the tub and watching the door handle. She stands and tips her beer up for the dregs, then drops the empty back into the meltwater.

Coming back down the hall at a shuffle, toes crunched up to make room for the wads of pills, she hears it. This big-animal huffing from one of the bedrooms. The door is cracked open a sliver. If Aiden notices her standing there, he doesn't show it. Doesn't stop, anyway. Keeps up his soft murmuring—hey now, there now, there—as though working to soothe a scared injured thing.

All through her life it will return to her—infrequently but faithfully—and most acutely in the loose hours of flight. The image of this girl, her body splayed across the bare mattress, her face puffed closed, dumb as bread. Lani standing in the aisle of a passenger jet, securing the straps of her demonstration oxygen mask, indicating the light on a life vest, placing the whistle mutely to her lips, miming serenity in disaster. Then a foul, chalky taste at the back of her throat, and there it is. Only a few seconds of it—the damp zebra-print underwear rolled down and cutting into the girl's pale thighs—before the door swings shut, the mind curtaining it again.

Peep show, she'll think, straightaway clenching her jaw at the comparison, perturbed. Coward, she'll think, for turning away at age sixteen and for not bearing to look now—at twenty-four, twenty-seven, thirty-two—when the scene arrives, as it always does, unsummoned

Once altitude has been reached and the seat belt signs have blinked off. After the announcement that electronic devices may be used if in flight mode. Once the stubborn meal carts have been shunted up and down enough times and the horde of passengers are adequately fed and watered, she will slip into a bathroom cubicle, press her hot forehead to the mirror, wonder if she's eaten something bad. All best intentions of bringing real food, fresh stuff, but somehow always the same foil-packaged bomb-shelter dinners as everyone in economy. She'll pull herself back from the mirror, frown at the smear left on the glass, and wipe it away with a tissue. She'll arrange the dark wedge of her fringe to hide all the trouble going on underneath, the concern etched there, paint over the tiny white scar on her lower lip in one of the airline's approved shades—red but not too red, not tarty. The jaundiced light aging her by half a decade. It's under such lights, several time zones from sleep, that her mother appears. Looking out, like some storybook queen, from the treacherous architecture of her own features in spite of the hair dye, the flicks of eyeliner, the brightened mouth.

Lani will buff her knuckles along the ridge of her cheekbone, as though grazing some heat there might soften the resemblance. She'll knot and unknot the rayon scarf at her throat, trying to make it sit right. Rinse at the taste in her mouth with a green, sugary wash. Spit. Spit again.

Her mother and the sprawled, benzoed girl; they will continue to find her there, suspended above the Pacific in that long-haul anesthesia, in a gloaming made of exit-row light. In the slept-in-clothes fug of mass slumber. These hours when her own body feels stateless, drifting mothlike from guide light to guide light, between the soft dings that summon peanuts and tonic water, but otherwise beholden to no one person, no one place. Beholden to nothing greater out there than the great dark that holds and keeps the plane. Earth far below, and real life down there with it, the self left unfixed and undefended. And so the ghosts float up, slip through.

•

In the first hours of 1991 she closes the bedroom door. Walks cool and deliberate as she's able, down the hall, heels snagging the carpet. Will is somewhere. She'll find him and tell him—what? Nothing, it's none of her business, and anyway she doesn't want to risk drawing attention to herself. She's tired, they should bail now, enough? She shoves through the screen door too hard, a bottle of clear spirit shattering on the concrete steps.

Fuck. Watch it. A girl scowling through hair dyed the blue of a sick Siamese fighting fish.

Lani turns and apologizes and tries to leave in the one action, her ankle swiveling, the step vanishing beneath. Face striking hard against the handrail, a warm, tinny taste spilling into her mouth.

The girl who's lost her vodka looking down at her. Hun, she says. You're bleeding.

Lani wipes the back of a hand under her chin, and it comes back slick. It's not mine, she tells the girl. Oh, it is. Ah, shit. I hardly felt it.

Here. Come on, you'll muck up your dress.

I hardly felt it, she says again.

Can she stand?

We're about to find out.

It's all right, I've got her.

It's Will, getting her under the arms. Watch the glass there.

Lani lets herself be lifted. Lets herself be led back into the house, like snapping back on a retractable cord, back to exactly where she doesn't want to be, limping past that still-closed bedroom door. No sound escaping now from underneath its sill.

In the bathroom she grits her teeth at the cabinet mirror. Red tracing her gums.

Will locks the door behind them—Lemme look—and Lani turns out her lower lip to show the split there.

Uh-huh, that could be worse. Won't need stitches, at least.

You a nurse now or something?

Might as well be. What with Dad. Siddown, can you? He drenches a hand towel with warm water.

Lani lowers herself to the edge of the bathtub, lets him dab at her chin, at her neck where the blood has snaked down. The towel smells of wet dog and petrol, and she tries not to breathe.

Don't know what you were thinking, touching his boot to her shoe. Accident waiting to happen, these; sure nothing's twisted in there?

Guess I'll find out later. If I take them off now, I might never get them on again.

Tilt your head back a bit.

Lani eyes the ceiling, its map of mildew. Feeling his breath on her throat, wondering what's keeping her from wrapping her legs around him. Only that she wants to. Someone rattles the doorknob and Will yells for whoever it is to piss off.

Pass me a fucken' beer, then. Whoever's mouth slurring up close to the doorjamb.

I said you can fucken' wait, Will tells the door. He folds the towel to find a clean corner, then goes back to his dabbing. She closes one eye to keep the fluoro tube from doubling itself.

Okay?

She nods and makes to stand to prove it.

Hold your horses, we're not done yet. He rummages in the medicine cabinet for a roll of cotton wool, tearing off a plug of it and running it under the tap.

Here. He packs the wool into Lani's lower lip. Okay. You look a bit like you're trying to start something, but the bleeding should stop pretty soon. You wanna stick around here or go?

Home?

'Less there's someplace you'd rather.

She might ask him now. *Could we go . . . Could you take me just as far as . . .*

And he might say, *Yeah, okay. How fast can you throw your shit together?*

But all that will mean is saving on bus fare, the little money she has stretching just a little longer. And she'd owe him something more than those few stingy bucks. More than she's already made up her mind to ever owe anyone.

No, she says. Sounding dopey around the soggy gauze. Just home.

The door handle rattles again, another fist pounding the bathroom door.

Okay. Let these munters get to their precious booze. Will flings the hand towel into the icy beer water, turns back to the sink, kisses Lani on her hurt mouth. Just procedure. He unlatches the door, but whoever was out there has given up and gone away. And when they pass that bedroom, it is empty, the door left wide open. As though nothing bad has happened in there. There's even a sheet spread across the mattress now, faded but tucked tight. Hospital corners.

Her helmet is gone, somewhere. Taken or lost, she doesn't know.

Will passes her his dad's old open-faced one—*blood bucket*—wears nothing himself. He judders the Honda over the ravaged road, not picking the way so carefully now: hitting roots and potholes, the bike jerking around like a spooked animal. Head-lamp bouncing crazily, sweeping deep into the silver trunks of the gums, signaling back to the wrecks out there, *Remember life?* Will keeps taking his hand from the grip to reach back and give a squeeze to her knee, and each time he does, she thinks, Now. We'll spill. And welcomes it almost. But it doesn't go that way. They make it out to the highway, wet-looking in the moonlight, gather speed, now and then the headlamp picking up the white bones of makeshift crash markers planted at the side of the bitumen.

Predawn gnats swat her face, and she swats back at them through the front of the helmet, swiping them away from her puffy lip. Her toes are crushed past feeling, for the sake of what? Twenty bucks, if she can be bothered to ask it, or her own little languor, a few furred hours to retreat into. Lani scrapes her heels against the pillion pegs, lets the shoes and their cargo fall into the road. A calm soaks in, with the warmth from Will's back, with every k put between her and that house.

One or the other of them howls. Then they both do. There's the moon hanging above them, looking one moment solid enough to knock on and the next moment like a hole punched through the dark satin sky. She keeps an eye on it, to stop it from darting away. Will reaches again for her knee, and she presses closer to stop the icy morning prying in between. Whatever she feels now is only because of the warmth from his back, the metallic taste of the early-morning air, and the two of them knifing through it. Only momentum, only velocity—how it settles something down in her. Still. The impulse is there, persistent and useless. The need to say one good thing, bigger than thanks. *May the road rise to meet you and may the wind always be at your back.* Just words she's seen somewhere, in cross-stitch—somebody's grandmother's busywork—but it seems about right. Then all of a sudden it doesn't. Sounds instead like a kind of curse—that first part about the road rising, what with the bike and all. The patch of skin on Aiden's calf, crinkled like plastic. She'd glimpsed that, she realizes. Looking in. The railway of scars along his leg where they'd stapled him back together.

She says nothing, feels herself floating out there in the dark. Beyond the reach of any of it. Hard and cool and distant as a star. It all belongs to this summer. A winter will come and roll over it, over Will and everything else, and soon enough it will belong to last summer. Then the summer before last. Three years ago, four. And after that she'll stop counting.

Creeping shoeless around the back of the house, she trips over the rabbit hutch, dragged up from the yard. They will outlast everything, these rabbits. Will still be there when both girls have fled, flown.

Her own bedroom window has been latched. No surprise. *You want to stay out all night, then by all means, my girl, stay out all night.* And she's slept out in the garage before, cocooned in paint-spattered sheets. But Ru. Ru will always let her in.

She doesn't even have to knock. Her sister's window has been left open a crack. Cat flap, Lani thinks, slinking in. Ru is already sitting bolt upright, liquid-eyed, watching her.

What happened to you?

Shh. Go back to sleep.

But your face . . .

Shh.

I wasn't asleep.

•

In the dark of her own room, she peels off the dress, stiff in places, sticky in others. Blood, dried and not yet. She steps out of her underwear and kicks around until she finds this morning's towel on the floor.

In the living room, her mother sleeps sitting up in one of the nubbly armchairs even though there's no one thrashing around in her own bed.

It's the infomercial hour, the ads just audible. People spruiking contour pillows, dinnerware, home-security gadgets.

Lani stands there a minute, wrapped in her towel, waiting to see what sort of free stuff they'll throw in. Waterproof shower radios, washable slipcovers, one for the home and one for the office, money-back guarantee. Stuff she knows is just useless junk, more plastic for fish to choke on a few years forward. *Secure it to the bench, and a little cabbage turns into a carload of coleslaw . . .*

It's someone's job, programming these dead hours, cramming them full. Someone's job to know who's out here, and that what they're lonely for at four a.m. is a home-beading kit or an ultrasonic pet remote, or sex chat lines, or Fred and Ginger dancing up and down stairs, up and down stairs. Crosby and Hope riding fake camels through a fake desert. Her mother loves that escapist shit, the ostrich plumes and the lit-up staircases, endings that are glamorous even when they're not happy.

The television light is not kind to her sleeping face, graying the skin, darkening the hollows. She looks drowned there, cold, in the underwater gloom seeping from the set.

Come on, you're gonna wreck your back, but Evelyn only murmurs a noise that sounds like agreement.

Lani pulls a red wool blanket from the armrest of the couch, where it's hiding a spot Belle liked to chew. Tucks it around the gray-blue ghost of her mother while on-screen a salesman throws in free steak knives, storage containers, pocket-size alarms. Things to make life easier, tidier, safer.

V
Madrugada

SOMETHING'S COMING. LES CAN SMELL IT LIKE WEATHER. CAN just about hear it, like a sound pitched so low that only the blood can recognize it. The dull thuds of homemade fireworks died away around two a.m., and then came a quiet spell, a brooding stillness now punctured by what's likely rifle fire. Just the odd crack of it now and again, beyond the fibro walls of the shed. Drunken New Year's rabbiting, boys who couldn't get laid now killing just to kill, whatever they can get. *Fill yer boots.*

He's been out here since one or so, working to settle himself. Solder smoke and citronella smoke mingling in the dome of light thrown by an old goosenecked lamp, hooded and twisted up like a bronze cobra. Showing Les his hands and the naked radio chassis upturned on the bench between them, and the soldering iron with its coiled wick. The radio's Bakelite shell stands sentinel beside the half dozen capacitors—waxy, dead—that he's snipped out, replacing bad for good as he goes. Plugging the radio back into the socket after each exchange, monitoring his progress. *A little louder, a little bit louder now*, the call-and-response of some old gospel number. Good good good.

He works in singlet and shorts, mosquitoes wreaking a pattern of havoc on his undefended arms and legs, never mind the citronella coils. A pause now and then to slap or scratch, or to etch the angriest of the bites with a cross, digging in his blunt thumbnail this way, then that. A trick his nieces taught him when they were little and still interested in showing him what they knew. The crosses are either meant to make the bites itch less, or they're to help the swelling go down. Or maybe they're only intended to shuffle the mind along; he can't remember exactly.

The radio innards give him the news—he thinks of bird entrails, of voodoo—telling him which parts of the world are just now rolling over into 1991: Hanoi, Jakarta, an hour-wide ribbon of Russia. That it'll be a fine day, thirty Celsius, no chance of storm. Les turns the radio off and fits it snug into its cover, then turns it on a final time, laying his hands on the Bakelite to feel the moment before sound arrives, that warm whir, as though it were a box of bees. Forty bucks, it'll fetch, maybe fifty. Or maybe Ev will like it.

He sets down the solder and rehouses the iron. Nudges the shed door and props it open for the cleaner air. Outside it's pitch, a velvet blackness. *Madrugada*, the Spanish call it. This dark stretch leading up to the dawn. English wants a word like that, something that sounds both magic and malevolent, but there isn't one. Or not one he knows of. Just *the wee small hours*, and that doesn't fit, doesn't conjure any of the right feelings, any of the wonder or the dread.

There's a stirring in the tall seeded grass beyond his fence line, a light breeze causing shivery spoondrift. *Gotta know your wind*, someone told him once. Years back, this bloke on a vine-yard job. Told it like Les was ignorant. He supposed he was, in some matters, philosophically and spiritually. His conversations with god amounted to little more than the transparencies of handwritten hymns looming up from the tabletop projector when he and Jack were Sunday school kids. And still, he'd only pretended to sing, mouthing the shapes of the words and letting the other kids fill in the sound.

But the vineyard worker wasn't necessarily talking about god. Where was this? Grapes. The Swan. Pruning instead of picking, so it couldn't have been later than September. The two of them working their way down the rows, doing only the left-hand vines so that the morning sun wasn't in their eyes—a system of their own devising. They'd do the right side when the sun had crossed to the west.

Look, the bloke was telling him, throwing clippings over his shoulder. It's simple enough . . .

There was a sort of guttering about his voice when he said certain words, an unsteadiness, the remnants of an accent. Les hadn't asked which part of the world it had come from.

You come to learn the difference between which wind is yours and which is not. Yes? Got it?

Les nodded, feeling all the while lost, and his workmate saw that.

Like with your hands there, he went on, gesturing with the clippers, and they both looked at the long-healed nubs where Les's index fingers had once been.

If you knew which wind was bad news, you maybe have seen this coming. You maybe have better prepared.

Les wasn't ashamed, but he busied his hands back among the vine leaves.

The fella went on: Someone else perhaps won the lottery that day. Someone else, perhaps he got his dick sucked raw—hah!—by some beautiful woman. Because that wind was his, but it sure as shit was not yours. So. You know which did this? He motioned again in the direction of Les's hands, the absent fingers, but what could Les say? It was as if they were never his to begin with, and once they were gone, he'd been relieved. There was no way of explaining that to the itinerant, to anyone who made a living with their hands. To avoid having to either explain or lie, he shrugged and grinned.

A nor'wester?

Shit, if it were so easy.

You said it was simple.

A boy came down the line with a barrow to collect the cuttings, and the man lowered his voice, as though his information was illicit, dangerous to too young a mind.

I mean, simple *concept*, he said, rapping his grimy glove against his temple. A simple *idea*. Yes now?

Then a bell had clanged, up at the homestead, for lunch. Doorstop slices of bread heaped with slabs cut off last night's roast, the meat sticky with mint jelly. The men pulled their shirts back over their shoulders and stalked up, silent, between the green aisles of vines.

Les doesn't know if it's true, about the wind, but it's something that has stayed with him. Like the crosses in mozzie bites. Like tapping the top of a drink can before lifting the ring-pull. Superstition, mostly. Habit.

This morning's wind is neither that which he supposes is his nor its nemesis. Just a skerrick of huff that has nothing to do with him. But it's carrying something along on it, sinister maybe.

He turns back a corner of damp hessian shrouding a crate of home brew, cracks one of the taller bottles, and swallows. Warm, overcarbonated, the heat over Christmas having brought it around too fast. For the past few weeks he's been heading out to the shed in the hottest arc of the day to swaddle the bottles with cool wet towels, trying to slow things down. Tended to them like crook little children, this batch of bottles (*get your own fucken' family*), but now here they are anyway, not too flash, but not poison. He raises the bottle in the direction of the rifle shots, then fills his mouth again with the failed lager. To the new year. Waste not, want not. Chin chin.

Yesterday Ev had come to him. At the burned-down end of the day, like fever dreaming. Appearing at the fence line close to dark, as one of his strays might, looking for he did not know what. From the kitchen window he'd watched her climbing under the top wire, stepping careful in her canvas sandals between the staked tomatoes and cucumbers as though she were trying not to wake them, and he wondered if she was onto him. He went out to meet her—sweat across her lip, her hair glowing white-hot, angelfire—then brought her into the cool and sat her down at his table and lied to her. Said no, nothing from Jack, when she asked him. She was apologizing to him in the same breath, saying she knew it wasn't a fair question, and he'd answered that it was a fair enough question given the circumstances, and they'd spoken of other things for a while, until she left.

There was more there, more to it than that, something stretching out languid and musky between the said and not-said things, so that he felt a traitor to Jack and Evelyn both.

He'd taken his brother's call early that same morning, stalking in from the backyard with the smell of oniongrass and fennel and mower diesel haunting his nostrils. And maybe it was the diesel or maybe sheer coincidence that had him already thinking of orange season when he picked up the bleating phone and there was Jack's voice. Accusatory at first.

Where the hell've you been? That's the seventh bloody try.

Les just about saw him there: an Acland Street phone box, with filthy words etched into the glass and the stink of wino piss. Jack lighting each smoke off the last, feeding in his change again and again as the line rang out, the poker-machine clatter in the refund slot that would make him flinch, each failure winding him tighter and tighter.

Doing the lawns, Les told him.

Mine?

Mine.

You been going over there much or what?

Just the usual. That seemed to satisfy him, though Les couldn't say why.

Christmas go okay?

Yeah, a real corker—what do you think? Les waited as the space at the other end of the line expanded to fill with sirens, tram bells, Jack's breathing.

Look, Jack said, I'm thinking of going up north for a bit.

What's north?

Oh, y'know. It's a bit like south, but your hat stays on.

Jack.

Mm. Yep?

And Les knew there was no point trying to talk anything like sense or responsibility into him.

Why even tell me? he asked. If you're not going to go where you're needed, you can go where you damned well like. Don't need my permission.

He waited—he'd a sense they were both waiting—for Jack to slam the phone down on him. But instead his brother cleared his throat and spoke: Thing is, I got a favor to ask.

Les was silent, waiting for the rest of it.

Listen, my passport? Thought I had it on me, but it must be in the trunk. You can send it to a mate in—

And Les told him to get stuffed, but he was already reaching for a biro and a scrap of newsprint to take down the address.

Passport. So, *that* far north?

I haven't really got it figured yet. Maybe just across the ditch. They've got boats you can take. And no snakes there, y'know? Sea snakes.

Won't go swimming, then. You'll probably have to chew the lock off it, the trunk. Can't remember where I stashed the key. Don't break a tooth.

Right. Anything else while I'm in there, your lordship? Really he wanted to state in no uncertain terms that this would be the last thing, the very last time he'd let himself be dragged into his brother's mess. But somehow the call ended with the two of them talking about Mildura, and the Goulburn, and an old joke about the Big Prawn, the Big Merino, and the Big Pineapple walking into a bar looking for the Big Banana—a kind of nonsense giggle their old man had told and retold, sometimes swapping out the Big things for other Big things—so that when they hung up, it was cheery enough, and Les stood there smirking for a moment before the fact of his idiocy caught him up.

He went, as he'd promised Evelyn he would, to haul the expired Christmas tree out to the roadside, and when that was taken care of, he let himself into the garage, tidying up a bit, knowing Jack would not be reappearing to berate him for doing so, then tinkering awhile with the bell on Ru's bike.

There's redbacks galore in there, Ru warned him, backlit by glare, the roller door lifted to kid height. She swiped her sweaty fringe out of her eyes and peered in at him.

I know, he said, demonstrating the bell while wheeling the bike over to her.

Dad'll get them when he gets back.

I know, he said again, feeling chickenshit. He watched her beat away, spindly legs whirring around lowest gear; then he pulled the door back down. On one of the shelves was an old vinyl suitcase—crammed now with tangled bundles of Christmas lights—that he recognized from the summer after the war. Was that a good summer? If there could have been a good summer so soon after Vietnam. And if it was even his brother who'd climbed up, plastered of course, onto the sleephouse roof and sang, crowed really, that ridiculous song about frozen orange juice, till one of the other laborers threatened to throttle him.

Oranges! he'd bellowed once more before clambering back down. God help me. Who knew you could get so bloody fucking sick of the little bastards?

Les felt differently, though, then and now; he still sometimes eats them the way he had in Mildura, where he'd made an art of it. He'd bang and roll them methodically against a tree trunk or the side of a barrel, careful not to split the skin, so that the insides were turned to pulp. Then he'd pierce the rind with a thumbnail (sting of citric acid on split cuticle) and suck the sun-warmed juice through the hole he'd made.

Like a mongoose with an egg, you are, Jack had said, his face screwed up sour. Jack always massacred his oranges, too resentful of them to give them any more of his time than he could help. Meaning he often just bit right in through the bitter skin and churned it all up together like a machine, hating every moment of it.

That season they slept on camp beds in the same long, low shed, partially shaded at their end by almond trees whose pink drift of blossoms covered the dirt, clogged the rain guttering. Huntsmen with the leg spans of railway clocks rested motionless on the fiberboard walls. Or motionless until Jack threw a boot at them and they danced up to the ceiling or fell maimed to the concrete floor, where Jack would proceed to stomp them flat.

They're harmless, y'know.

Bugger that, nothing's harmless. Jack gave his sleeping bag a few violent shakes to unhouse whatever might be lurking there.

Each night they fell onto their beds, sagging with muscle ache and with beer from the Worker's Club, a few words volleyed into the dark and returned across the four feet of empty space between them.

Hey, 'member the house in Doncaster?

Doncaster. With Vin Frisk?

Uh-huh. Frisky Vin . . . those magazines.

So what about that house?

Nothing, really. Just thinking aloud I s'pose.

Then silence, or what passed for silence in shared quarters. But Les could count on one hand, not even requiring the index nubs, the number of times he actually caught his brother asleep in that shed. Sometimes he thought so, with Jack lying as still as death itself, breathing inaudibly. Then the glint of his eyes would give him away. More often he'd wake to Jack sitting upright, watchful, staring out the one grimy window or else standing on the other side of it under the almond trees and cupping the glow of his cigarette. Keeping it hidden, although there was no longer reasonable cause for that. Not as if this were high school and old Mr. Barnard was going to come juggernauting around the side of the shelter sheds to scruff him. But Les understood why, and he saw his brother, his half brother, standing there under the dripping pink trees and knew he'd be cupping the glow for the rest of his life. For the rest of his long, watchful nights and even the bright days strung between them. Hiding the light of his smoke from men who may well be dead by now, or were in any case thousands of miles away, across land and sea both, and more land again.

He'd heard it said—of men their father's age, of men from other wars—how so-and-so never made it back. Not to mean that so-and-so had died over there, or even that he'd left pieces of himself behind in the gangrenous pits dug by makeshift hospitals. Rather that a different man had come back in so-and-so's place, riding in his body and speaking in his voice, but staring out through the mask of his face as if with a different set of eyes.

Not so with his brother. Jack had come back home as himself but with the war in him like a dormant, cancerlike sickness, busy at some cellular level. Perhaps blooming there in the soft tissue the whole time, all the while they were tipping back schooners at the longest bar in the world, only giving itself away in the smallest of actions—in the clench of his jaw when the bell clanged for last drinks, in his watchfulness and his cupping the glow.

Boys came home from that war and took a test as if for drunk driving. Got a penlight shone in their eyes, got asked to locate their nose on their face—Close enough, son—and were sent on their merry way.

Les had watched him out there, blowing smoke into the almond tree branches as if maybe there was something up in the leaves he meant to flush out. He may've been thinking about the war, or he may've been thinking about Evelyn, the reason he'd come along. He'd said he wanted fast money from work he could just as soon walk away from, said that was the only kind of work he ever wanted again.

I thought girls found it sexy, the projectionist gig.

I'll tell you what's not sexy. Earning bob-fifty an hour and kipping in a sleep-out.

You won't make much more than that picking citrus.

Yeah, but I'll make it faster. And the tax man won't get a greedy bite of it.

He didn't talk much of Ev that season, or of the plans he had rattling about in his head, but every few nights he'd try calling her from town. Leaning at the pay phone outside the pub, toeing the mica-flecked footpath like a kid. Scratching her name into the booth with a shard of bottle glass while he waited to see who picked up in that big old house on the central coast. If it was Mr. or Mrs. Morgan, he'd hang up right away. But that early on, he couldn't tell between Ev's voice and her sister's, on the phone at least, so sometimes he'd get in a *Hullo, stranger* before Stell brought the receiver down on him in the way she'd been instructed. He'd come moping back inside then for another tall glass of *fuck-it-all*, staring down into his beer like it was a hole leading to the center of the earth. It was only a couple of times that he got the right girl on the line, and on one of these rare occasions the two of them nutted out a code. He'd give three rings, then hang up, and she'd know it was him, that he was thinking of her, and that would be enough.

Les had wondered then, What if someone picks up before three?

I told you. It's a big frigging house.

What was it about her? Les remembered the last girl, Jody, how he'd had to listen to all Jack's elated raving. Knew even the useless bits: how she stomped on her lacy things in the shower, called everyone she didn't like Francis, and was shadowed relentlessly by a red spaniel, once her grandmother's, who would only obey commands leveled at it in Welsh.

But Evelyn was a blank card. Hardly any point asking outright, though, curious as he might be. Jack just pushed his hand through his sweat-stiff hair, long grown out of its army crew cut. Said, She doesn't want too much from me. Les thought maybe he knew what that meant, though years later he'd dropped by unannounced and caught them in the midst of a row, Ev backed up tight against the bathroom door, Jack's fist knuckling her chin as he frothed over with the filthiest words he could think to call her. Her eyes were closed, and although her lips were motionless, it still looked to Les something like prayer, the way she was. Something almost serene about it, unearthly, as Jack pulled his fist back and pounded the door beside her head—*What do you people want from me? What do you people want from me?*—and the plywood splintered at the third blow. Les could've walked in on a dozen worse scenes, he knew (there was evidence enough of those, in the house, in Ev's face), but this was the one he'd stumbled into. Neither one of them had noticed him there, one hand still stupidly clutching the bunch of beetroot he'd pulled up from his garden to make a present of, to trade for company. Then Ev opened her eyes and saw him there, and Jack turned, and Les didn't know the strength in himself. He got his arms around his brother, and the smell of the man was fearful. Not a work sweat or even a brawling sweat, but an acrid, cat-piss panic, ammoniacal, as though he truly believed he might die there in that dim hallway, where there was not a thing that wished him harm. They fell together onto the mottled carpet, Jack twisting like a possessed thing inside the poisonous slick of his skin as Ev stepped to the other side of the smashed bathroom door and locked it. He let go of his brother then, holding his palms out even as he staggered to standing, but Jack, quicker to his feet, only looked at him and spat, disgusted, onto his own floor.

Get your own fucken' family. Then he'd left, taking nothing, and Les knew better than to follow.

Ev? He spoke with his mouth close to the splintered plywood. You okay?

No sound came from the other side. No answer, no sobbing. Then the running of the shower. She came out ten minutes later, wrapped up in a towel, and looked surprised to see him still leaning there, the beets propped patiently by the baseboard. She brought a hand up to where the towel tucked in between her breast, and kept it there. All her makeup had been rinsed away, and she looked at once old and childlike, her hair damp and pasted to her skull, smelling of kids' fruity shampoo.

Go home, Les, she told him, and moved past him down the hallway, into the dusky gloom of the bedroom.

Certain moments would lose substance in their revisiting, memories he'd meant to preserve instead rubbed back to the oily sheen of overhandled suede. Les sometimes struggles to hold true, for instance, the lightning-struck tree flaring up like a torch, spectacular, burning alone on a dark hill outside Bendigo. Or the baby shark he and Jack had caught for a pet, shepherding it toward a rock pool where it would be stranded when the tide pulled back, so that they could simply come back later in the afternoon and shoo it into a bucket (Mim had said no way, obviously, when they marched it proudly up the beach).

Or how, not long before she tried to drive them into it, his mother had called him to the bank of the river (when he remembers it, it's the Tarwin, though he cannot say for certain) and pointed to the water, to glinting flecks amidst the silt, and they had worked for some minutes to scoop them up in their hands, the flecks always evading them, swimming between their fingers until finally she realized—or was it himself who saw it?—that they were grabbing after the reflections of stars.

That, too, is murked and shifting, deteriorated like overplayed video.

But this is something else, this blue in the hallway. This has held clear and sharp, unwavering, years after the fact. And he believes it's owed to this: when Jack's fist slammed again and again into the hollow door and then through it, an inch from Evelyn's face, she had not flinched. As in a side-alley show, some knife-throwing act, she had not flinched. And in a way Les understands this to be worse than all the violence he did not witness, worse than things he only ever saw in aftermath.

If he's honest with himself, Les is afraid of the trunk, of what he might find in it. Though his curiosity nearly won out months ago, when Jack first brought it around. (He'd seen it coming then, had been planning this disappearing act at least that long. Since August? September?)

The girls are getting arsey, he'd explained, looking everywhere but at Les. They're into everything, the both of them. I had it stashed up in the roof of the garage, but nowhere's good enough now. And these dropkick mates Lani brings around . . .

No worries, plenty of room here.

And you won't, y'know . . . You won't either . . .

What do I want with your fucking Viet love letters? So that both men could laugh. Not real or easy laughter, but close enough, and together they shifted the bastard thing from out of Jack's Ford and around the side of the house. Jack had already known him for a yes, then, arriving with it on the Ford's back-seat. Les himself already sensing that an ask was coming, that this was about *something* when he saw Jack pull into the drive, or else why wouldn't he have just walked over as usual?

You got this thing up and down from the roof on your own?

Don't ask. Think I earned myself a hernia.

Les looked at the jerry-green footlocker, remembered it hunkering in the hallway at Dad and Mim's. Dinged-up and paint-spattered, the strap snapped away, *Puckapunyal* stenciled in white, hurried work.

Want this inside or out?

Damned if I care.

Les didn't ask *Why not just get rid of it then?* but instead pointed with his chin through the back door and into the spare bedroom, where there was nothing but an empty aquarium and several decades of *National Geographic*.

Would anyone know it to look at?

Might, Jack said, and so they threw a sheet over it, piling on a few stacks of *National Geo* for good measure.

There you go—love seat!

How long since you looked in it?

Dunno. Years.

You even know what's in there?

Yep.

Everything?

Just about.

Like what?

A wigwam for a goose's bridle.

You mean it's none of my friggen' business . . .

None of your friggen' business.

Les figured it sure as hell looked to be his business, from where he was standing, but he left it at that. The padlock would've been simple enough to get around, just a pin tumbler, but it would be easier still to take the lid off its hinges. Which he nearly did, some hours later, hovering about it with a Phillips head, feeling like a bee or a hummingbird, before thinking better of it.

Now that there's permission, he's even less keen. Since Jack's phone call, he's been steering clear of the spare room, whether he needs something from it or no. Has felt the trunk throbbing in there, and never more loudly than while Jack's wife sat at his table, turning the sugar bowl around in her hands, having already asked what she'd come there to ask, but not knowing how to best get away.

Finally in the room with it, he realizes he's still listening for something, realizes how absurd that is. He leans his weight on the cutters, and the lock jumps apart. Les steels himself for horror. Gruesome trophies, souvenirs. Leathered, unidentifiable flesh threaded onto bootlaces. Teeth and hair. He'd heard tell— well, Jack had told him—of how they'd smuggled back all kinds of bizarre mementos: creatures, both living and taxidermied; all manner of crude weaponry; virility potions of exotic plant matter and ground-up crawlies. And keepsakes of their own dreadful devising.

But inside the trunk there are no such atrocities, or at least nothing that speaks of them in any language Les can understand. Opening the lid, he's met with a mildewous fug; the must of jungle or roofspace, he can't say which. On top, a chemist's envelope of photographs: twenty-four prints that show, over and over, the same six-by-four-inch rectangle of milky blackness. A film that hadn't been threaded properly in the first place, Les guesses. Had stayed curled up snug while the shutter snapped on god-knows-what. Beneath the photographs there's other paper paraphernalia. A few pamphlets. Manuals. *Soldier's Handbook for Defense Against Chemical and Biological Operations and Nuclear Warfare.* An Agent Orange info card. A sketch on the back of an onionskin leaflet. This was Jack, he saw, messing around with a rifle, either dismantling it or putting it back together. A few letters from home. One from himself:

I reckon Dad and Mim have already told you about the NT trip. Practically prehistoric, this place, crawling with dragons. Goannas, I mean. Have you ever seen those pricks up close? Last night we watched one go after a chicken, and it was carnage.

He remembers that time, but not writing about it. Remembers who he'd been including in that *we*, but had otherwise seen fit to leave unmentioned—that tall Darwin girl, Elena, her sweat like dry wild sage, like dust rising from a narrow track above the sea. Commando under her damp Levis when he finally shucked her out of them. He had known, he'd thought, what he was doing, kneeling on her crumpled jeans, the high ridges of her hip bones cupped under his palms. But she'd laughed up there, above him, amused but not unkind. Said, I'm not a mango, sweetheart, and he'd tried to rein himself in a bit.

She'd been the one to talk to, about his mother. Or perhaps the need to talk had arrived, and she'd simply been there to hear it, the blackened shells of pilfered abalone piled on a sheet of newspaper between them and a tallboy of rich stout passed back and forth.

There were only two years stretching between the first memory of his mother and the last. All of it badly vignetted, interspersed with a great lot of highway. Riding in the backseat, being handed back salty packets of things, paper-wrapped things. Quick leg stretches around country war memorials. A police officer rapping a torch against the driver's side window, Can't sleep here, love. And her voice soft outside the car, which had meant that they could, all right, this once. The two of them at the edge of the river that final bright, hot night, trying to scoop out stars with their hands.

He had understood, at the bridge, what his mother meant to do. She'd turned around to look at him there, in the middle seat, had given him that conspiratorial smile she kept for him only. Her eyes as brilliant as living coral, and he had not been afraid.

The rest is not of his own remembering; has since either been told to him or he's overheard. How the river was tidal, low enough at that time to do no great harm. That a man out walking his dog had seen it all happen and had run down the embankment after them. That she was a bit cut up, and Les was a wee bit shaken, of course, poor lamb, but at the end of the day . . . And it's a miracle, really . . .

And so to his father then, and to Jack, and Mim, who had cause enough to hate the sight of him, but never seemed to, or never showed it, having perhaps learned of his existence years before and being, as she was, a pragmatic sort. He in turn would think of her, always, as Dad's Woman. Some residual, senseless loyalty he could never argue himself away from.

They'd never taken him to the home she'd been put away in. It wouldn't be healthy. So said Mim. And later, when he was old enough and able, he hadn't gone himself, and she had died in there not too long before he'd written Jack about the goannas, leaving out his mother and the things he'd recalled for the girl, for himself, amidst the fire-roasted abalone and the companionable stench of charred shell.

And it's true what they say, about the beaches here. Jellyfish season! Saw this little tacker just about drowned in vinegar . . . Anyway, hope the wildlife's friendlier where you are.

He folds his letter back into its envelope and tucks it among those from Dad and Mim, from Jody and Nan and whoever else. Farther down in the trunk there's camping gear, tools, a rubber groundsheet. Random women's things. An NVA shirt still packed in brittle cellophane. A crudely whittled chain of three complete links, with a fourth cracked open. Any medals, Les knows, are long since lost to hock shops, to drink; whatever's in here is all there is to make sense of who his brother was for that humid, useless year.

The set of jungle greens are folded neat at the bottom, keeping their creases. In the pocket of the trousers he finds an envelope, printed with the address of their Warrandyte house, the moss-green weatherboard where Mim still lives, alone now. Recording old movies off the television and talking up at the possums in the roof, as though the creatures are saintly. Foul smells and stains of them seeping down through the plaster of the ceiling, causing a putrid cartography.

They're not hurting anyone! she'd hissed when Les offered to remove them. Humanely, he'd promised. But she wouldn't have a bar of it.

That address. Stamp of a Roberts painting, rams being sheared. Return address to one R. Fox, number of a post office box in Bundaberg, QLD. Too heavy to be the passport, and in any case postmarked June '74, with the seal left intact, untouched.

Jack hadn't been curious then, must've known all along what was in there. Or else hadn't wanted to.

Les studies the careful print of his brother's name. Considers steaming open the envelope to discover what its rectangular bulk might be, but instead—bugger it—slides his thumbnail under the gum-sealed lip and rips it ragged. The cassette tape he shakes out is half played through, labeled in the same neat hand. *CB (May) 1968. First Light.* That's all. No letter keeping it company.

The only working tape deck he has these days is the one in the truck's dash, and even that is sketchy. He sets the cassette aside.

Unfurling his brother's shirt, he feels a greasy dampness settled in the cotton and the weight of dog tags tucked into the breast pocket. He leaves the tags clinking there, slides his arm down into the sleeve, cautious, as though something might've taken up residence. One of Ruby's infamous redbacks. But his hand appears at the other end, unbitten, the cuff falling inches short of where it should, halfway to the elbow; he stands nearly a full foot taller than Jack, when he's actually standing straight. Had his mother been a tall woman? He couldn't remember. There are a couple of photographs he was given, but none that gave any frame of reference, none with anyone he knows. None with his and Jack's father, of course. But Les believes she must have been. A stately woman.

There's no mirror in the house save the one hung up to shave in front of, a disk that could show him little more than his jaw and the safety razor moving over it, carving swaths through soap lather. In any case, he can see as much as he cares to reflected in the darkened window—the room and himself standing in it in his brother's too-small shirt, looking enough of a goose.

Would he have gone, if his numbers came up? *If your balls got yanked.* He might have. Or he might have just gone bush, left the silly buggers to fight in a war that had nothing to do with them. But then maybe his hands really would've kept him out. *Conscientious cowardice*, people thought. And there were better, more courageous stories he might've invented—shark attacks, gambling debts—but he let them have that one. *Can't pull a trigger without a trigger finger.* Because, though they thought him strange for it, or worse than strange, the truth would've had him straitjacketed, loony-binned.

It was never a simple matter of dislike. They looked all right. He supposed they'd be fine on someone else, wriggling at the end of a different pair of hands. That was just it, though—they weren't his. And they disgusted him. That was the simplest way to explain it.

He disliked his voice at that age, and still does—how it rises and wheels away from him sometimes, the way a very young man's might. Shrill. But he's never felt the compulsion to sabotage his throat, to ruin his vocal cords gargling drain cleaner or what have you. He might have smoked his way to a more pleasing gruffness, that would have been easy enough. But truth is that he could never be arsed. It was never what you could call an *imperative*. He just speaks as little as any given situation might allow. Understands that people who do not consider him a placid and patient man think him a humorless, suspiciously private man, and he's never taken pains to influence them either way.

The fingers are another story. The fingers were an imperative. The inversion of a phantom limb, something that should not be there, but you look down and there it is—there they were—and each time the fact of them perturbed him.

He was only, what, a little shy of twenty at the time. In a way he's proud of himself, that kid, how sensible he'd been about it, understanding it wasn't a thing to rush through. *Measure twice, cut once.* He'd given himself thirty days to chicken out, marking them off on a pharmacy calendar for 1967, a photograph of the Daintree Rainforest that flipped over to the Great Ocean Road at day twenty-three. October, November. That final week of red-penciled crosses picketing the white boxes beneath the picture of limestone sea stacks.

When the day came, he leaped at it, volunteering himself for a morning of clearing and splitting deadfall on Nan and Pop's seventy acres before fire season swept through.

You're a love, Mim said, and packed him a lunch.

The right and then the left, he'd decided the night before. Was there a workable logic to that? He was right-handed, and figured that the second go would be shakier, that there'd be the shock to contend with. An unsteady right was surely more reliable than an unsteady left. Well, he didn't know if that was so, but he didn't want to risk buggering it up. Didn't want to just wound the hateful things; wanted them gone, both. The first one and then the second. The right and then the left. That easy. He'd had his lunchbox filled with ice and a flask filled with Bundaberg, and a couple of rubber bands he'd taken from around a bunch of asparagus. Sparrowgrass, he said to himself, wondering if this should be funny as he waited for the skin below the knuckle to turn bruise-colored.

The sound came as unexpectedly bloodless, the hatchet biting neat through bone and sinew and sticking fast in the stump of the red gum tree. He had thought he'd feel faint, but no. Just plunged his hand into the waiting lunchbox, half ice and half water now. The ex-index finger rolled off the red gum chop block and lay by its lonesome in the dirt, and Les kicked a clump of leaves over so that he wouldn't have to look at it there.

A kind of calm flooded in to fill the space, immediate and bodily. The right thing after all, the right thing. Or maybe it was only shock. Whatever it was, it was usable.

With his left hand he lit and held one of the cigarettes he'd rolled before the act, and it was the last time he'd ever hold a smoke that way, though it was no longer even natural to do so. He'd stopped using the offending fingers whenever possible, and it had become his habit—when nobody was watching him too closely—to hold a cigarette or a pencil or his tableware pinched between thumb and middle finger, ring finger taking up the brace work. But it seemed important, this idea of *last* (he'd understood himself then, already, as a man of small rituals), so he smoked in his old way for a couple of puffs, watching the left index finger losing color and warmth below the rubber-band tourniquet. Then he shifted his smoke to the edge of his mouth and planted the left hand down starfish-like on the tree stump.

Les shook his right hand from the ice water and, gripping the hatchet handle with the remaining fingers and thumb, was aware of the unfamiliar distribution of tension; he felt the new span there, and the compensative work being done by his wrist muscles. Beautiful.

All the time in the world, he thought, steadying himself, though in truth he'd stopped feeling that there was. The sense of urgency was not attached to his own feared squeamishness, but to the possibility—the fair possibility—that someone might happen on him out there, by accident or design, and would intervene.

No one did.

When it was all done, he made sure to fling both of them deep into the scrub, not caring where they landed, lest someone send him back to hunt for them, to force him to have them sewn back on. A warm drizzle started falling then, turning fast to drenching rain, and it seemed further testament to the rightness of the decision—for who would fairly expect him to cut timber in a storm?—and he drove himself the twenty klicks to St. John of God Hospital in a downpour, feeling he'd just gotten away with a heist. A good wind that day, certainly, he could've told that Swan Valley vineyard worker years later, if he hadn't by then learned to keep his stories on the dark side of his teeth.

Light coming into the sky now, turning it crepuscular. That isn't a color, but it should be, Les thinks. Crepuscular blue, crepuscular pink. People would know what you meant. Something piscine about it. Isn't just him who thinks so. The sun's setting and rising, it's always the color of—always has something to do with, in any case—fish. Salmon, that one's easy. Or the undersides of mahimahi, the gradients of blue-green-yellow. He feels drowned by it all. By the light spilling into the new year, and by measuring the distance between his own understandings and the understandings of other people.

He folds Jack's shirt along its creases and returns it to the trunk, to its matching trousers. Everything else still laid out on the carpet to show the order it had been exhumed in. Wartime strata. He fits everything back as it was, lingering over a tortoiseshell comb, running his thumb over the teeth to hear the purr. When the failed photographs are back on top, he slams the lid on it all. Only the cassette is held back, radiating with weird heat in the back pocket of his jeans.

No passport. Jack would only be getting so far, for now.

Halfway out to the truck, crunching down the drive, there come the rabbiting shots again, a patter of them at some distance, then a few pocks nearer by, as if by way of reply. The whine of dirt bikes like thin wire strung between them. Les pauses there in the drive, listening, the cassette feeling like a wad of too much cash; then he turns instead for his backyard, the bottom fence line, where sometimes needy things—old foxes, lame crows, a cancerous feral cat—will come stealthily from the grass to take whatever small offerings he might leave there for them.

Along the ridge, he sees them: two bikes stitching back and forth. A marksman behind each rider, sitting pillion, taking potshots into the long grass. Or no, not potshots. He sees now and then the tap to the rider's shoulder or thigh, a signal to slow. They've got something out there, though nothing he can see. Then he does, or believes he does; there's the path of its flight, sashaying of the seeded grass giving its game away.

What are you devil-shits after?

He thinks then of the feral cat, the gray face gnarled in tumor. Its wet breathing and the terrible snacking sound of its eating when he was close enough to hear. He figured he'd shoot it himself when he thought it time. The thing was determined, you could see, to live, and he didn't think it his place to tell it otherwise. Not yet, at least, and anyway not like this. Though all along part of him has reckoned it would turn up shot one day, his cat. Strung up on someone's barbwire in the usual manner taken with foxes and the like, both trophy and warning at once.

He's standing there, his hands wrapped around the taut top wire of his fence, and the boys see him standing so. One of the pillion-sitters raising his rifle in something like a salute, and the other leveling his, bluffing. Or is this a kind of greeting in their parlance? Les doubts it.

He names them, the shooters—Angus Ferran, Jimmy Knox— shouting their names up to the ridge. And he too is bluffing, no true threat to them. They're setting to leave in any case, bored now or spent of ammo. They churn the ground up in their leaving, to save face, a violence they mightn't have seen cause for had he not called them out. Les watches the riders giving throttle to the bikes, hooning up and down his fence a couple of times, close enough for him to see through the open faces of the helmets—Aiden MacCallister and another he does not know, some city cousin perhaps.

He'll go out there in a little while to look for it. Thrash his way through the sea of grass, combing it, methodical, for whatever it is they may have maimed or killed. His cat. No, not *his*, exactly, but somehow; he's beholden to it. In better light, he'll go.

But he feels, then, his blood beating in him like a sea at spring tide, pulled by what force he does not know, overreaching its own line of drift. And he understands to turn, to see—the dark shape of something heaving in the sage. And then no longer heaving, simply there, motionless. Catlike, he sees when closer, but it's not his doomed tom with the malignant roses blooming over his snout. And not—or not logically—his brother's panther, the captured mascot, the one Jack had come home emblazoned with at age twenty, grinning like a prize fool at the fresh ink under a blood-tinged slick of Vaseline. Not that cat either.

This one is no bigger than a Doberman pinscher, full-grown but stunted and runtish, in- or crossbred to the point of ill-construct, perhaps the last descendant of some rickety line. At once wonderful and pitiful to see there, superimposed on the wrong landscape, patchy hide stretched over a poor frame.

When her side finally falls flat and does not rise—when he's sure it will not rise again—he ventures a hand to brush a flank, feels the rabbit shot, both recent and old, riddling the flesh beneath the fur. Dusky coat bearing her old cat scars, her old cat stories. A congregation of cattle ticks have not yet abandoned the exotic settlement of her ears, though they soon enough will.

Whatever secrets she's carried with her this far, she's leaving them beneath the drought-thinned arms of the sagebush. *Her*, it's occurred to him, though he doesn't check to make certain. Likewise, the eyes, he would like to know—are they a luminous, oily gold? A dull, oxidized green?—but they're lidded over, and he doesn't intend to impose his curiosity on the creature.

He leaves her there a moment, returning with a crackling tarpaulin woven of mud-colored plastic. Lining up the edge with the animal's spine, he tucks the tarp between the grass and the blood-matted fur. Her mouth is rigid in a frozen snarl, mottled pink-black gums bared. The teeth, Les sees, are the grayed yellow of old tableware, those ridged bone handles. Taking hold of the cracked forepaws (no quiver of the partial snarl, and the eyes stay sealed), he turns her onto the tarp, exposing her hurt side, learning the nature of that hurt. Not the smattering of nuisance pellets, but two metal bolts protruding from her shoulder and throat. He'd not seen the crossbow, only the rifles. He's sorry to leave them there, the bolts—it seems to him wrong, somehow, that a body should go to the earth still holding what killed it— but they don't twist away from their homes as easily as he'd hoped, and all at once he finds he doesn't have the stomach for it this early in the day. He covers the panther-thing over with the remainder of the tarp and pulls her across the yard, out of reach of the day's oncoming heat. Anyone watching him—and people are waking now, must be, staring glassy-eyed and headachy at the detritus of last night, the sticky tables still crowded with plastic cups, relatives and overnighters crimped up on too-small couches—anyone who happens to see him now would figure it only a cord of wood he's dragging, or engine parts or a dismantled motorbike, to the sour shade beneath the veranda. He weights the edges of the tarp with old palings and loose paving stones, a barricade to keep out any of his nosy visitors—the crows, his tomcat.

When dark comes, he'll bury her, though Jack's girls would hate him to know of it, would feel betrayed—as might Jack himself—what with Belle.

Sorry, he says aloud, though he doesn't know to whom. An old tic, *sorry, sorry,* before he can even determine the source of his guilt.

The truck's cab has a brackish smell to it, at once stagnant and salt—or that's his own stench, unslept and unwashed, and he's just trapped himself with it. His hands, at least, are rinsed of panther grime. And he feels awake enough, buoyed on a raft of unlikely materials, a volatile energy thrumming in his chest. He rolls down the driver's window, but whatever breath the earlier morning had is spent now, the day airless and silent, as though domed over with glass. He drums the cassette, recalls the last album the Holden's tape deck chewed up and spat back at him, unribboning: *Down in the Groove.* But in a way it had been right of it to do that.

Would a bigger man listen or not listen?

At first he thinks there's nothing. Clicking play on the A-side and waiting several minutes, hearing naught. Then, near the five-minute mark, a bird pips. In the recording or in the world— the trees outside his truck? Les rewinds and listens back, and there it is, a bird, or something like it. Some minutes later there come voices, too low or too far away to know which words or even which language they belong to. Other noises, intermittent, unidentifiable. And, a little way out from the end, a man clearing his throat—had he been there the whole time? Had he crept up, silent? Someone clearing his throat, as if about to speak. Then nothing. Or almost nothing; the sound of the record button being depressed. The sound of a mind being changed. Sound of there being nothing to say.

He flips it to the B-side, where there is only virgin static, but Les sits with it anyway, to make sure. Looking out at the road for the occasional vehicle straggling past his house. Unfamiliar faces peering back at him from unfamiliar cars, radio antennae angled toward god and newer wars.

{How It Sounded}

OCEANIC, A GREAT, DARK SWELL, SOURCELESS.

Sometimes, yes, like great wings. Some terrible feathered god-like thing beating the air close to our faces.

Like iron wheels grinding along a clay road.

A clock ticking under soft cotton, something an orphaned animal might believe a heartbeat, be made calm by.

A thick weave of birds lifting into the sky all at once—as a blanket shaken out—and then settling back just as they had been. Only the leaves shivery and the sunlight stirred to say that anything had happened at all.

The tearing of fabric. An old silk jacket ripped open along the seams.

Twang of a slack wire. A low electrical murmur.

Big machines cooling, tok-tokking like geckos.

Trees dripping mist, sweat rising to steam.

And sometimes like a voice. A low, sweet voice of no discernible language calling us from one room to the next.

VI
Fire Plan

FEBRUARY OF THE ALMOST FIRE, ALONE WITH ONLY YOUR mother in the house. Deep into the runout groove of summer, with even the Gulf War winding off. *We now return to your regularly scheduled . . .* But the fire plan was full of holes—Lani, Dad, Belle. All of them so newly gone that it hadn't occurred to draw up a new one yet. You still had the old plan printed neat into an exercise book:

Open the gate for Belle. She will follow because she is a loving, faithful animal . . .

Then a checklist split into two columns, two colors. Your responsibilities and your sister's. But by the time the fires arrived, it was just you and Mum and a box for the rabbits. And when you reached the edge of Norm Hornett's muddy reservoir, even Uncle Tetch wasn't there waiting. He was already away, looking after Grandma Mim, as she was starting to go strange.

The fire was close enough to see, though not all that ferocious. Mum had brought along a blanket, rolled up and tucked
beneath her wing in case the wind suddenly swung around and
you had to wade out into the slimy water, cuddling rabbits, with
the red wool drenched and held over your heads for a flameproof
cubby. But the fire didn't swing, and never threatened to, so
Mum shook the blanket out and spread it on the ground instead.
That made it like a kind of picnic, sitting there at the edge of the
dam. A bag of fruit and a transistor radio. Sharing bites of apple
with the rabbits, who didn't seem especially frightened. Just
shuffling about each other, nibbling at the corners of the box
now and then to investigate its strength. Maybe they weren't
smart enough to be panicked, though the air was smoky to
breathe. Or maybe they knew better than you did, because the
fires weren't so bad that time around; all people lost were a few
sheds and fence posts, a bit of grandfather-tree shade.

Mum flung herself back on the blanket with a sigh, scuffed
off her dusty canvas sandals. She was wearing a pale blue cotton
dress, something that would've looked proper on a very old
woman or else a very young girl, and there was a ladder creeping
up from the toe of her stocking. She'd been wearing the dress all
morning, but when had she thought to put on hose? You worried
it might be a sign of insanity, dressing up for a bushfire as though
it were a special occasion.

She propped herself up on one elbow to look at you. Kind of
peaceful, isn't it, Possum? We should do this all the time, you
and me. Then she looked back over her shoulder at the rising
smoke and went on, Only without the burning trees.

There was a small, strangled noise in the back of her
throat, a whimper. Then the laughter that cracked out of her
was so convulsive, you thought you might have to run and get

someone. Her eyes already wet and her shoulders shaking violently, she made shallow animal grabs for breath when the laughter would let her, while you stood by, helpless. Like watching somebody drown a long way out from shore. Where had it come from? Perhaps the smoke in the air had starved her mind of oxygen. You put a hand on her knee to remind her you were there, felt the trembling in her leg. The laughing went on for a while, finally puttering down to a few stray coughs; then she cleared her throat.

No, she said, brushing invisible grit from her dress, composing herself. We should and we will. Bugger those other two. Reckon we've earned ourselves a bit of fun.

Of course you never would—there would never be any cause to—but you sat there together for another hour or two, tracking the fire and waiting for the all clear. Watching the sun turn the red of molten glass as it sank toward land, in and out of the haze.

Nothing more beautiful than a bushfire sunset, she said; isn't that mean, in a way? Then she rolled up the blanket, grass seeds and all, and you carried the rabbits back across the paddocks to the strange stillness of the house, where Lani's bathers still lay scrunched up in a corner of the laundry sink, stinking of pool chlorine and lately of mildew.

For weeks your mother had gone out of her way to work around the bathers, putting them to one side when she needed to hand-wash something, then putting them right back as they were. She insisted that you leave them be as well, that your sister could clean up her own mess whenever she came slinking back. Finally you couldn't stand it anymore. They'd dried out, mummified in a stiff tangle. You bundled them into a plastic shopping bag and hid them in the kitchen bin, camouflaged them with food scraps. Mum never said anything.

You went through a full year of high school wearing your sister's clothes, left-behind things filched from her dresser drawers. Ripped op-shop silks over Tencel denim. Men's shirts. Heavy silver jewelry, tarnished black. Your mother eyeing you warily whenever you slouched into view, all jangle and glitter and soot.

You look like nobody loves you, Ru.

For a while the clothes still smelled of Lani's sweat and her cigarettes, and of the men's aftershave she'd nicked from somebody's brother. Cool Water. You held the material to your nose and huffed, were careful to never spray anything over it, but the scent wore off eventually anyway. Then an American rapper went and put it in a song, and soon everyone was wearing it. For years afterward, boys leaning in shop doorways or mooching in sharky packs at the train station would make you think of your runaway sister, your heart shivering whenever you caught the familiar combination of cigarette smoke shot through with the bright mineral cologne.

Once, your mother busted you taking the cellophane off a new box of the stuff.

Where'd you get the money for that?

They were selling it at the chemist. Your voice held convincingly steady.

That doesn't answer my question, she said slowly, and when you refused to say any more, her open hand was there, trembling in your periphery, hovering like a kestrel about to dive.

You stood firm, already taller than she was, staring her down. Go on, you goaded.

She spoke through her teeth, but she lowered her hand.

Ruby. Love. You're a good kid. You're loyal. You're my last good thing. Don't let me down, hey?

And by then you understood that *loyal* was a kind of snare, felt it cutting in like a wire looped around your ankle. You surrendered the cologne so that she could return it.

In later stoushes, her hands flew instead to her own hair and tore at it with such a violence it was as though it did not belong to her.

See what you're doing to me, girl? See now?

You saw.

Well? Happy?

You thought maybe you would've preferred to cop the slap.

Go on, just hit me then.

Go on, just leave me then.

Are all family scripts so interchangeable?

The first woman you fall in love with says, I want to know everything about you. She says, Show me how, then wets her fingers in your mouth. The first woman you fall in love with reads you poetry as though she is inviting you into a box she has built and lined soft with her voice, a bed she has made warm with her body. She coaxes your childhood out of you in scraps and flashes, with deft cat paws. Never whole stories, but true enough. Fragments you try to lathe the sharp edges from as you tell them, so that she can listen without flinching, without having to say, *Oh, sweetheart*. The sounds through the wall, but not the blood in the sink. Sketches almost small enough to unsay. Small enough to tuck behind your tongue, to swallow.

Tell me how you were when you were younger, she says. Tell me something fun.

You tell her what passed for fun in the town you grew up in. It always seemed to involve destroying something. Your sister driving wreckers into dry creek beds just for a bit of a jolt, just to make something happen. Limping home at fifteen with a piece gouged out of her knee from where the ignition key had crunched in.

She's quiet for a while, this girl in the warm dark, like maybe you've talked her to sleep. But she's only waiting for the rest of it.

Your sister? But I was asking about you.

Oh. Well, I don't know. I feel like I was about the same.

More silence, then her small, sharp *Huh* before she comes out with it—First boredom, then fear. As though she's finally figured you out, reached a diagnosis, and is prescribing something that might help. Larkin. She likes to quote that other one too, about parents and how they can't help but mess a person up. But you've met her mum and dad, she's taken you home to them: wry, generous people with a lot of cashmere and stoneware under high-vaulted ceilings. An oncologist who keeps bees and knows everything about their intimate customs, and a retired cartographer with vivid stories about trekking the Tigris in the '70s (*When I was by that great river the Tigris . . .*). You know their house smells of books and woodsmoke and the persimmons left to ripen along the kitchen windowsill.

You do not tell her that you feel like a tourist in this house. But what you feel is just that. Hands in your pockets, as though fumbling for the cost of admission.

When she says to you, First boredom, then fear, you do not correct her. You do not tell her, *No, first fear, then boredom—I think something in us just calcified.* (That closed fist still throbbing behind your ribs; so much for growing pains.) You pull her closer, stroke the inseam of her arm until she and her questions and answers fall back to sleep.

•

In the end it takes a twenty-foot skip to hold it all. Boxes of crockery and rolled-up posters, suitcases she doesn't bother to look inside. Your old beat-up bike. Armfuls of bed linen, as though somebody had died of plague. Again, you wonder if she's lost her mind.

Are you just going to stand there, Ru?

Yes, you just stand there. Cradling a mug of tea by the front steps, watching it all go in. Uncle Tetch handling the bigger things, the shabby furniture and boxes of unlabeled videotapes.

Salvaged: a cigar box of cicada shells, packed carefully into cotton wool. One balding flock mama deer. A box of cologne, still packaged in yellowed cellophane. Talismans. Unusable things. You tuck them into a shoebox and tape it up and mark it *trousseau*. A strange little joke you'll tote unopened from one house to the next.

Occasionally there are notes. Postcards showing foreign cities. Your sister, killing time in the airports belonging to these cities, choosing pictures that show monuments and natural attractions she may or may not have visited herself. Occasionally you are moved to trace a plane across the sky, glinting up there like whitebait. She can go all that way, travel all that distance. Slipping back and forth across meridians, across the dateline as if it isn't so much as a crack in old linoleum. Hours flooding in or tumbling away like scree. But you haven't seen her face since she was sixteen, chlorine stiffening her hair, the cut still healing on her lip.

•

Then Easter Saturday, years later, half waking to her weight at the end of the bed. Your sister has become so light, at first you think: Cat. That one of them must have snuck in, sprung up.

You are twenty-two years old, and she has driven all night, through bad weather, to reach the bayside address she sometimes scrawls in childish loops. The house she finds you in holds seven people, ghost odors, faulty wiring, suspected asbestos. Cupboards full of stolen glassware and instant ramen. When trains rattle past, this house shakes its window casings like rickety fists, coughs plaster dust from a network of fissures. Families of stray cats take refuge in the overgrown backyard, and while the more tenacious ones occasionally move inside, mice continue to run their skittery cartels behind the walls. It's the first place you're able to call *home* without your stomach clenching, and it will be knocked down for apartments within the same year. Your room in it is large and bright, with most of the floor space given over to rolls of canvas and silk mesh, milk crates of paint and ink, a narrow daybed pushed into the bay window. At certain times of the year the light spills in underwater-green through the new soft leaves of vines, but when your sister shows up, the vines are bare, the light untinted.

The impression of her there, through your eyelashes. Backlit by too-early morning. She's propped the window sash with a tin of linseed oil, is breathing smoke out into the thin winter light. Bottle-black hair banked over her face. Still wearing her uniform. Or no, you'll see later; just a shirtdress all wrong for the season, but half asleep, you mistake it for cabin garb.

Even with the window open, the room has filled with her smoke, and it carries into your fitful half sleep, becoming that of the fires: that first year, boiled-wool blanket spread by the dam, your twelve-year-old self clutching fistfuls of summer grass to stay anchored in that summer, to the scrape and thump of rabbits shuffling in their box, Mum cracking up over nothing. These sounds as loud as if in the next room.

For a flicker of time, Lani exists in both places, like those double-sided trick cards whose images merge when the card is twirled around fast enough. The horse and the rider becoming horse-and-rider, the cage slamming over the bird. Your sister is there by the window and she is there by Hornett's dam, her long legs stretched forever, stretched toward the water. But looking as she does now, nursing the hot drink that somebody from downstairs has given her, fiddling with the knot of the silk scarf that is meant to go with her hostess dress. The still-sleeping part of you wants to grab and hold her, keep her there, whatever fight she might kick up. If you could just get the two of them into the same place, Lani and your mother, then perhaps—

But it's ten years since you've seen her. And there's the grit of a hangover waiting behind your eyelids, stymieing generosity. Why should she be let off easy, allowed to waltz right back like nothing's happened? The part of you that is awake demands to know, Who let you in? Who gave you that? then shifts the pillow to block out whatever the response might be. Remembering her bathers growing mold in the laundry sink.

It's no use; she's still audible, still there in spite of the buffer of musty feathers and yellowed pillow slip.

Kiddo, she's saying gently, shaking your foot through the covers. Come on. I didn't drive all this way for a cup of orange pekoe.

•

Outside, it's very cold, very clear now, with the fierce metallic light that comes after a night of storms. Crossing the park, you can still taste last night's party. Lychee vodka. Never again. Ancient eucalypts have dropped their gnarled limbs throughout the playground, and the area is taped off like a crime scene, deserted.

Apocalyptic, Lani says, wind snarling her hair as though it means to haul her up by it.

True. Which horseman does that make you?

Her car is unbeautiful, a gray, froggish thing nearly as old as she is, its interior a mess of takeaway containers, rumpled clothes, paperback thrillers. Airline miniatures of toothpaste and gin. A battalion of near-empty coffee cups, the gut-rot stuff from pit stops along the Hume, milky dregs curdling in spite of the chill.

Pestilence, obviously, she says. Peering into a coffee cup and wrinkling her sharp nose.

Thought you'd drive something else. Sleeker, you tell her, standing there curbside, shrugged into a silver puff jacket. Couldn't you have just flown? Don't they let you fly for free?

Tired of flying, she says, sweeping rubbish from the passenger seat. Climb in. Don't worry, it goes. How many weather balloons died to make that jacket, Ru?

Haha. You slam the door.

The radio comes on with the engine. Talkback, a comedy quiz show with a guest politician. She switches it off. There's an odd smell, familiar and foreign at once, thick behind the smoke-filled clothes and the phantoms of woodsy air fresheners. Something grassy and cloying.

Lani meanders the car around the edge of Port Phillip Bay. Yacht club, surf club, bowling green. Are you hungry, she asks? We can stop somewhere if you like.

No. Let's just get to wherever we're going. Where's that?

I didn't really have any place in mind. Just the drive.

We're not actually going anywhere? You swivel in the passenger seat to search out the smell.

What're you after?

Nothing.

If you're hungry, there are some snacks in the glove box. She reaches from the wheel, springs the catch on a muesli-bar cemetery, empty wrappers glinting among road maps, broken sunglasses, pamphlets for winery tours. A duty-free cache of American chocolate and European cigarettes.

Oh, right. That's for—Happy Easter.

The chocolate or the smokes?

Anything you like.

You're bribing me? I'm not five. And though you don't quite mean it as a joke, she laughs, flashes her crowded-out incisors, the faint scar on her lip.

Anyway, you got it backwards, you tell her, tearing the cellophane off a random soft pack. It's supposed to be European chocolate, American cigarettes—everyone knows that.

She brings the heat up and you wind the window down, letting in the scent of the rained-upon inner suburbs, now waking—damp air laced with exhaust fumes and turning kelp, drying bitumen, Vietnamese bakery. You want, for the first time in years, to feel that sugary bread sticking soft to your teeth. Remembering impromptu picnics, waiting for traffic to thin, your father fresh out from the repat clinic. Mum at the helm of his old Ford. Hot pies and dense pastel meringues eaten in city gardens, watching aggressive swans hiss at toddlers. Watching your father, white paper bag trembling in his big hands, pastry flaking his new whiskers. He'd be drowsy in the passenger seat for the drive back, a flicker of how he might become as an older man, gentler, grown too tired for rage. Was she waiting for that, your mother? And could that be called patience or plain idiocy, or did love allow room enough for both?

Lani murmurs a song you don't recognize as bayside apartment blocks flick past. White stucco, pink stucco, all their blinds open for the view, display-case living. A cream linen suit hung up in a third-floor window, waiting for someone to fill it. Race day. Lani asks about art, and you tell her. She asks about men, and you correct her.

I did know that, she says, accelerating to make an amber light. It's so much easier to talk when we're driving, don't you think?

In the backseat, her silenced phone growls and growls and growls, but she doesn't reach for it. You want to ask who's calling, who her life is made up of now, what kinds of friends, what kinds of parties. What she's done with all those years. How she answers when people ask where she's from. Whether she's happy: rarely/sometimes/often? But your mouth refuses to open for those questions. Out of pride and something else. Loyalty.

I got a dog a couple of months ago, she's saying, prattling now, filling space. I don't know, maybe that's selfish, since I'm away more than I'm home. But a friend traded up for a baby, and it was bye-bye, Bruno, poor old fella. The neighbors all love him, though. I thought of bringing him down for the ride, but you might just as well bring a buffalo. Actually I did see that once, a buffalo, only it was on the back of a motorbike. All trussed up, crazy. That was Laos, I think.

Lani?

Mm?

Does Mum know you're down here?

Lani lifts a hand from the wheel and rolls her wrist. Yawns. A stalling technique you remember from when you were young. It does for an answer, and in the long silence that follows, you take inventory of the glove box, keep your hands busy coaxing holiday brochures into three dimensions—swan, lotus, peacock. A modest repertoire of serviette origami you learned setting tables in a suburban Thai restaurant. Your sister ignores the dashboard menagerie. After a few more ks she sighs and flicks the indicator, swings the car across the oncoming lane and into a green place, oceanside. Cypress trees dripping wet crepe streamers from Good Friday celebrations, and tables haunted by ugly, thuggish seagulls hunkered down into their feathers. No one's around yet, and the gulls stand mobster-like along the railway sleeper benches, eyeing the car ruefully. One lands on the bonnet before the car has even stopped, peering in through the windscreen. You hold out a piece of chocolate for it to see, and it cracks its yellow beak against the glass, streaking birdspit.

Lani kills the ignition. From where she's parked, you can see down the beach to the breakwall, the few colored plastic buckets stationed along it. People flinging lines out into the wind-riffled bay, casting for who knows what. Jelly blubber and toadfish.

You smooth a failed lotus back into a Margaret River winery map, determined not to be the first to speak.

Lani watches you level the creases. It was different for you, Ru, she says. You were too young to really . . . Look, she was just different with you.

The smell you noticed earlier is stronger now, without the air rushing through the car. A peculiar animal must to it. Not a doggy smell; greener than that. You swivel around in the passenger seat again to scan the back. Two plastic shopping bags are stuffed behind the driver's seat.

What're those?

What? She twists to look. Oh, they're wool. The lanolin reeks a bit, doesn't it? Sorry, I've stopped noticing.

You reach back into one of the bags, tug a greasy strand from the bundle, and roll it between your fingers. What's it for?

I don't know yet. A woman was selling it outside her hobby farm on the way down here. From her own lambs, she said.

They'll be chilly, though. It's the wrong time of year.

I wouldn't know. But she looked cold out there herself. Frail. I felt bad for her.

You tease the wool strand to fibers. But not Mum.

How do you mean?

You don't feel bad for Mum.

Lani straightens up. Oh Jesus, sometimes I do. And sometimes I still feel angry as hell. Other times I don't feel much of anything—I go to picture her face, and something in me just blinks off. Is that awful?

You shrug. Yeah, maybe that's worse than angry. Is it the same way with Dad?

I don't feel all that much about him either. I don't think I do.

You don't *think* . . .

Well, you know, every now and then I'll see someone. From the back or the side, sitting in a parked car. Waiting outside a terminal. And from the way their shoulders are set or whatever. How they're holding their ciggie. It nearly knocks my breath out. I don't know what that says. Of course I'm always wrong, anyway, I see that as soon as they turn around. And a few months back—but he'd never fly, right? Said it always made him sick, even when he was in the army. So I knew all along that this wasn't him either.

•

In the story that your sister tells, the man who could not be your father boards a red-eye in Perth with a gray duffel, a heavy cable-knit cardigan stretched across his broad back. She says she cannot recall exactly what it is that first draws her attention to him over the hundred other passengers. She has been awake for fifty-something hours, and life has taken on a dreamlike, under-water feel. And as in dreams, every encounter seems luminous, important. These are the times she's dumb enough to buy lotto tickets, when she hears a thread of wisdom in the things the Dar-linghurst crazies rant at her from their putrid doorways, from their nests of rags and paper. She knows, you both know, that this is only a hereditary delusion.

The man with the duffel is tall, folded uncomfortably in spite of his exit-row seat, in the manner of one who has come to accept a certain amount of discomfort. He's taken off his cardigan and rolled it into a bolster for his back, and when Lani comes by with the drinks trolley and asks what will he have, he smiles at her in a pained way and says, Just tonic, dear. Little bitta lemon if you've got it.

Dear. Not *love.* A woman's word. Or a more tender word anyway, she's thinking, pouring his fizz into a plastic cup and spearing a slice of lemon. When he reaches out to take it, she sees the tattoo, just the hindquarters sticking out of his rolled shirtsleeve, the splayed claws, the flick of tail. She might have seen a thou-sand men with blotchy big cats climbing their arms, but this is different.

She's staring hard enough to leave a bruise, but the man with the tattoo doesn't seem to notice. He takes a few deep swal-lows from the tonic and leans his head back into the seat, closing his eyes. Someone two rows along is already badgering her—do they have iced tea? Do they have lemon squash?—and she trundles the cart to a woman with a couple of brats whining for cola.

When she goes back through the cabin with the snack trolley, the tattooed man is already asleep, bulky cardigan pulled across himself for a blanket, his arm covered up again. Then the lights are dimmed, and the other passengers angle themselves into similar impressions of sleep. She decides that she will say something, about the tattoo. Upon descent. Or maybe before, if she catches him awake. She'll find the right moment and keep her questions innocent, impersonal. Just curious. What it means, and so on. She won't go and embarrass herself, or him, by asking outright: Did you know my father? Or maybe she will. Maybe she will be that brave.

She makes excuses to walk past him for the rest of the flight, springing up whenever somebody hits the call button, but he sleeps on. They're somewhere over the desert when one of the engines gives out.

Oh, all the time, Lani says when she sees your eyes widen. Happens all the time; they're pretty much made to fly with just the one, and the engines are built so that no one but the pilots know when something buggers up. Still means an emergency landing, though.

The real chaos doesn't start until they disembark, swarming a tiny shelter shed of an airport on the brink of civilization. All the rerouting to get sorted, everyone inconsolably held back from east coast business meetings and honeymoon cruises and dying great-aunts and farewell stadium shows for retiring entertainers. The man from the exit row never enters the clamor, never raises his voice. He sits patiently with a tabloid newspaper by the window of the crummy lounge, taking occasional bites from a vending-machine chocolate bar. But somehow the right moment never arrives, and before she can say anything, they're ushered onto different planes.

Lani's quiet a moment, rolling her wrist again, as if to crack it. Down on the beach, a couple of kids stamp through a tangle of sea grapes, rabbit ears fitted over their woolen hats.

That's it?

That's it, she says. Finito.

You let him go. Without even . . . It's not a fair question, but she answers as though it might be.

I can't help feeling like maybe I wasn't meant to say anything anyway. That maybe speaking to him wasn't actually . . . wasn't the point.

The point? You're being superstitious again, Lah. The nickname like a foreign object, there in your mouth after so long.

I know I am, she says. I'm only saying what it felt like. And probably it was just something off a tattoo parlor wall somewhere. Straight off a wall, where any old goose could ask for it.

The wind carries up laughter and the crackle of burst sea grapes, like someone snapping their fingers, lost for a word.

What was it—the last straw? Was there a last straw?

I don't know, she says. Jeez. Maybe the dog—that was rough on him.

I meant for you.

Oh. Because you want me to say I'm sorry.

Not now. I don't really give a damn anymore. But yes.

Okay, she says, but still doesn't say it.

One day you will tell her. How her absence eclipsed his absence. How he vanished completely when she took off. But this afternoon you are either not big enough or not small enough to say so, and she drives the eight hours back to Sydney without hearing it. Five months after, she steps off a plane in Port Hedland and refuses to step back on. She lets her hair go the color of a baby mammal. She gets pregnant to a ranger from Esperance, and they name their children for places they hope to one day see. You post small gifts to the west coast. She sends back photographs of the gifts being worn or held or chewed on.

It remains mysterious to you, how you were mild and she was savage. Way back there. But somewhere in the years between, she must've used her anger up, run herself to exhaustion. Burned it all away like quick, hot fuel, flaring high and blinding, then gone, smokeless.

You wonder when your real life will start. You wonder what good all your being good has amounted to.

One morning you flick on the radio, and there's a report about recent studies in genetic memory, the inheritance of lived experience. The studies consist largely of torturing mice into fearing the smell of cherry blossoms, so that their offspring might also fear the smell of cherry blossoms. The baby mice are satisfactorily terrified. Beyond reasonable doubt. They get a whiff of the synthetic blossoms that were piped into their fathers' electrified cages, and they huddle together in a trembling gray mass in one corner of their safe little unwired room.

Sometimes you'll look down, and there are your fists, clenched. You just find them that way. An involuntary action, though you suspect that some part of your brain does this voluntarily. Purposefully. And although you don't entirely grasp its reasoning, you do hold theories.

Here is the hippocampus. Here is the amygdala. Here is involuntary motor control . . .

Something it doesn't want you to look at, something that is within its best interests not to see. The tail of something fearsome disappearing around a corner. What's hiding in there? What are you so afraid to look at? But your fingernails spike your palms before you get a chance to follow. At the first whisker of something you might remember, you scarper back into the corner of your cage.

It doesn't make any difference, turning away like that, doesn't put a stop to the howling that surges up in you sometimes. From somewhere unknowable, a dull echo there in your blood. The sound of great wings, of iron wheels grinding along a clay road. Old Terrible. And because you do not open your mouth for it, do not howl, it moves through you in other ways, comes out in sweats and tremors, the way it did your father. A violent shaking that takes you to the bathroom floor, cheek pressed to the cool, dirty tiles while you wait for it to be done with you, to roll over and away like the black cumulonimbus chargers of coastal storms. The dreadful grandeur of it almost ridiculous against the backdrop of crumbling grout, spilled aspirin, the stray flattened slipper lost beneath the soap-scummed claw-foot tub.

Twenty minutes burn up. A full hour. All the while this feeling that you might be throwing off light and heat, emptying out brilliantly, like a star collapsing. Thinking, This time. If no one comes. This time, I will die.

But then, simply, no. No one comes, and you do not die. You run a bath and fall in and stay there until the water is cold and your lips are colorless, until there are doors slamming downstairs, voices rising from the kitchen, strangers and friends. Then you get out.

You keep waking from those dreams. Where the dead come back to get a look at you, just to see what the years have done to your face. Always the feeling of leaning back against sun-warmed brick, lulling and simple and familiar. The sweet, heady mingling of magnolia and lawn mower fuel. And it's fine for a while, all the catch-up talk. *Tell me, love, just what're you looking forward to?* How cheeky her kids are getting, and how soon the water restrictions might lift.

Everything looks a bit parched, tell the truth. Tell the truth, I'm a bit parched myself. But can't complain, really, can't grumble too much, hey?

And aside from that thirst, no word or hint of death. The cheeks not sallowed by it, the eyes still alight. But after a while you feel it must be your place to quietly inform them—that it's only polite, the way you would for someone who'd left a zipper undone—that they're not alive anymore.

You're sure everyone has this dream, or some version of it, sooner or later. That it must be about as common as the one with the falling-out teeth. Only more difficult to make sense of, because the dream with the teeth means pretty much the same thing for everyone: *Looka yonder, change a-coming.* Whereas the dead always come back to tell you something specific, particular to you—isn't that how it goes?—only they'll never tell it to you straight. You want to grab them by the shoulders and shake it out of them. *What do you want? What do you know?* You try pressing them. But the dead just smile, like they're humoring you. The dead go all aloof and change the subject. Ask whether

Arnott's still make those biscuits they liked with the coconut. And when, dumbfounded, you tell them no, not for years (*have you really been away that long?*), they seem to have more trouble making sense of this than the news of their own mortality.

That long? I s'pose I have, love. I suppose so.

If he is dead, someone would come and tell us. Never you mind. And if he wanted to be found, we'd know that too.

But did you look?

Did I look. Ru, you tell me: How much looking did I do? How much running after? Were you asleep all those years—were you dreaming, girl? Your mother, turning her back in the kitchen of the blank suburban unit. Easy-clean venetians, nothing on the table but a bowl of lemons and the big ginger tomcat stretched out across the racing form.

Anyway, she says, ministering gentle half twists to the cat's lionish ears, What's got you to thinking about him all of a sudden? Bet you my last dollar he's not thinking about us. Wherever he is. Off in woop-woop.

Oh, I don't know, you tell her. Scraping at waxy lemon skin and yawning in the way Lani might. I guess they were talking about Father's Day on drive time coming over here. That was probably it. I don't think about him all that much. (This is one kind of loyalty. Another is: *She didn't say to say* hi, *exactly, but she did ask after you.*)

Here, you say, sliding a photograph onto the kitchen table.

Your mother looks into the photograph, nods at some private question. Asks, without looking up, Which one is which?

The one patting the quokka is Alyeska. The other one is Skye.

She nods again. Later she slips the photograph between the pages of a cookbook she rarely opens, children's cakes.

At some point during the course of her fifties she'd come back into the stern Scandinavian beauty she'd started with, albeit a little taut now, a little lived-in. She takes a long, unhurried time putting herself together in the mornings. Her lips lined and filled, silver-blond hair twisted up tight into a marcasite barrette. For her own sake, she says. No more *I used to be*. Now she is again. Like being written back into an inheritance. Only now there is nothing much to do with it, no worthwhile place to spend it. She waves a hand when you ask if she isn't lonely.

I was lonelier when your father was around. And not as if either of you girls needs a father now, anyway. (Still saying *girls*. Still that stubborn.)

Though men look at her now more than they ever did, or more than you ever remember them doing. You catch them at it, standing apart from her in public. Even in simple clothes—the blue cotton sundress from the day of the fire, decades old and taken in and taken in—there is something. There in the guarded grace about her movements. Something compelling. Selecting stone fruit at Trang's Grocery, cupping her slender hands over the downy cauls of peaches and apricots so lightly she might be testing their warmth. Carrying herself with the same grave care, as if walking with a very full dish of water she is determined not to spill, never to spill.

Perhaps preoccupied with that task, with not spilling, she seems farther away than when you were young. Farther away than she was in her rages, her fierce disappointments and hair-tearing.

In her bathroom you scrounge the cabinets for evidence, medications that might hint at her cooling, her pulling away, but there's nothing at all to incriminate or explain her. Even the walls of her small house are left blank, painted a glossy china white, like the inside of an eggshell. No pictures, not even a tack mark. As if to say, *Look; nothing happened here! Nothing ever happened here!*

But at times when she's concentrating, lost in thought, you'll see her tongue seek out the gap he left in her teeth. And now and then his name appears in the search history of the old PC Aunt Stell set her up with. You don't need to follow the links to know that not one of them will arrive at him, that Jack Burroughs is only a dragnet of far-flung solicitors and dentists and wedding photographers and motocross heroes.

When the two of you drive north to visit Tetch, you listen: Does she also hold her breath while going past the old house, they way she always said to do with cemeteries? (*It's impolite to breathe in front of those who can't*, she'd say, but you felt the real reason was something else, if no more rational.)

As for yourself, yes, you hold your breath. Old hurts and petty thefts long buried in the yard. Dirty words you etched into hardwood stumps, lying on your belly in the sour under-house dust. The roof tiles that stained your feet red, then broke beneath them. These are still there, and it might be they will hear you, and be woken.

Viburnum has grown up to screen it now. Green-and-orange-striped sunshades on the front windows, like gaudy eyelids. Evidence of a different family strewn about the lawn, a family's worth of gumboots ranked beside the front door.

Even so, you still half expect to see one of your own there, captured in the flicker of kitchen fluorescents or hauling up the roller door.

Your mother, staring from the passenger seat, she never says, *Look* ... She never says, *Remember when* ... Though her eyes might scan the lawn, the lined-up boots, the trike, the red heeler pivoting, barking out at the road, at your black sedan.

We're late, as always.

He won't mind, my heart. He never minds.

Always, there are offerings stationed by your uncle's letter box, spillover from his garden now that there's no one to help him eat it. Recycled ice-cream containers heaped with plums, apricots, oranges. A note saying *Please Take*. Though half the time they end up being lobbed right back at his truck, sticky rinds candied to the windshield. He'll put the next crop out there anyway. *Help Yourself.*

Why?

Stubborn, I s'pose. He shrugs. Don't let the bastards drag you down and whatnot.

Your mother talks to him the way she used to talk to the rabbits, but only once you've left them to it, sipping at their glasses of cloudy shed-brewed ale. Strange itch to it, like swallowing grass seeds. Their faint murmur following you out to where you wander between the crowded garden beds. Cucumbers and capsicums, tomatoes with their stalks noosed to stakes by ruined panty hose—Blue Midnight, Silken Mist—that your mother has worn out and saved for him. If there's more to it, you don't want to know about it. You break a pea pod away from a lattice, crunch into it, taste drought. Spit it back into the mulch, where the yellow bones of some animal or other are poking up through the loose earth.

Tetch will try, once again, to send your mother home with cuttings he salvaged from the magnolia before the new people cut it down to extend the old house. He equips her with perlite and peat moss, margarine containers of hormone grit, handwritten instructions for coaxing the roots, but nothing ever takes. She tucks each new endeavor behind the laundry door to shrivel up black inside its makeshift milk-jug greenhouse.

Still, somehow, the spilled salt thrown over your shoulder, even in restaurants. Still counting the magpies in the cypress branches, as though a higher *Something* has taken the trouble to arrange them out there for you to tally and make sense of. Still your heart slipping whenever a sparrow finds its way into the house, whenever a forlorn ornament stows into January.

By the time you meet your nieces, they are already upright, flanking your sister in her doorway. Leaning into her shyly, just to feel the reassurance of her freckled hands in their soft hair.

Say hellow, she tells them. Be polite.

All through the gauzy, jacaranda bore-water Christmas, whisking up purple blooms instead of pine needles, there's your sister's sweet voice singing between rooms, Who's my Tiny? Who's my Bewdy . . . and the girls careering down the hallway by way of reply.

You sit out on the deck with a drink in your hand, turning the glass, letting the glass grow warm. A tourist, even here, watching her children running under sheets of sprinkler mist.

I was so afraid at first, she says. Low-voiced, as though some-one else might hear and misinterpret. I was so afraid there wasn't enough good in me to make anything good. That I couldn't . . . not biologically, but whatever else a person needs. You know?

You tell her yes, you know. Telling yourself that yes, this is where you're meant to be. That you might yet shake your dis-trust of any thing, any love that comes to you easy, palms up.

Telling yourself to be still, to let the day billow like sailcloth, and the days that follow on from that. (*Did we make it?* you want to ask. *Are we here?* That mythology you once read, about children who start as splinters in the heel of some mother-god or other, how long it takes them to work through the skin.)

New Year's Eve, she's pulling the blinds open on the pewter light of late afternoon, the power blown by a summer storm.

Tell me that's not an omen?

Love, it's not an omen. Her gentle man, shaking his head: another hour till a taxi will nose down the wet gravel drive, that white, downy corona through tinted cab glass.

He stands by the open back door, thumbing emergency D-cells into an old radio. Scanning past the hit parade and sports commentary to reach the World Service, the shipping bulletin prattling out low and steady. You listen, the five of you, making a game of it for the girls while the television is temporarily deposed. Everyone lying almost still and almost quiet on the living room floor, reverent during the litany of meteorological predictions for these faraway storybook-sounding places: Viking north at zero south at zero southwesterly veering northwesterly five or six occasionally seven later perhaps gale eight later wintery showers good occasionally poor Forties Cromarty west veering northwest five or six showers good ... Thirty miles one thousand and one falling slowly northwest three seven miles nine nine nine falling slowly Ronaldsway west northwest three sixteen miles nine nine nine falling slowly Malin Head northwest five showers five miles nine nine nine ... Now rising, and the girls clambering giddy onto furniture so as to rise higher. Taking turns at swooping toward their father's chest, then into his arms from various launchpads, from armrests and chairs.

Now falling—help me down!

Now rising—help me up!

They can make a game out of anything, these three, Lani whispers, reaching for you across the hardwood floor. And I was so bloody afraid . . .

Falling slowly—help me fall slow!

Now rising!

Feel her hand close lightly around yours. Rising. Okay, yes. By some latent grace. The heart unclenching at the memory, at the echoed sensation of stepping into the stirrup made by someone's (*his?*) interlaced fingers and having them *hup-hup-hup!* you weightless into the stinging, silvering air. Caught there for a moment, suspended, like a star between the grainy sky and sea. (When was that? And if you could press that moment flush to this, what might slip between? What might fall away, be lost?)

You think, Here. Please. Let her find us just like this.

But the remembering is spooled away, the thread snapped. The girls fall once more into their father's arms as the broadcast turns to headlines—West Africa is falling, crude oil and the ruble are falling. Greece is still falling. Only sea levels and the U.S. dollar are rising—and the man whose shoulders you flew above vanishes, now as always. Here again is the hardwood floor, like smacking back breathless to the glassy surface of the ocean. Dried blue husks of jacaranda blooms swept in under tables, behind chairs, amidst the household's dust. Your sister letting go your hand and getting up in time to see her, out there, making her way across the soaked lawn. Stepping ginger-footed through the confetti of blossoms crushed into the grass and stone, as if a parade has only just passed by.

Acknowledgments

Several organizations have contributed invaluably to the development of this book and to my practice as a writer. I gratefully acknowledge the generosity of Yaddo artists' colony, Arts Victoria, the Australia Council, Omi International Arts Centre, the International Writing Program at the University of Iowa, and the Wallace Stegner program at Stanford University.

•

Deepest thanks to Jonathan Lee and all at Catapult for seeing a U.S. readership in this, and to Claudia Ballard, for long-standing faith.

Ongoing thanks to my Australian editor, Ian See, for your patience, intuition, and acuity through many earlier versions of this book. Thank you, Madonna Duffy and UQP.

Thank you, Tobias Wolff, for your guidance and generosity, and for encouraging a longer endeavor. Thanks to Elizabeth Tallent, Adam Johnson, and Daniel Mason for so much care and counsel, and to my fellow Stegners.

Acknowledgments

Thanks to Ocean Vuong, for allowing me to borrow lines from the superb "Someday I'll Love Ocean Vuong" for the epigraph. Thanks, David Astle, for the cryptics in "Breakwall."

Thanks, Lang, Ash, Krien, and McKay for early insights. Thank you, Chris Flynn, Robert Skinner, and Angela Meyer, for being so sturdy and transpacific in your friendship. Thank you, Judith Hamann.

Thank you, always, Patrick Pittman.

References

"Breakwall" includes excerpts from the following texts:

Harold Holt, Vietnam Ministerial Statement, October 17, 1967.

Robert Menzies, Vietnam Ministerial Statement, April 29, 1965.

National Service Registration Office, conscription letter, Department of Labour and National Service, Sydney, 1967.

Royal Commission on the Use and Effects of Chemical Agents on Australian Personnel in Vietnam, *Final Report, July 1985*, Australian Government Publishing Service, Canberra, 1985.

United States Department of the Army, *Soldier's Handbook for Defense Against Chemical and Biological Operations and Nuclear Warfare*, U.S. Government Publishing Office, Washington, D.C., 1967.